DRAWING LEVIATHAN

MIKE CHINN

SALADOTH

PRODUCTIONS

SALADOTH PRODUCTIONS

Hall Green, Birmingham
United Kingdom

I would like to express my thanks to Peter Coleborn and Jan Edwards for their patience, help and assistance in preparing this publication.

Dedicated to the memories of Richard Basehart and David Hedison. Every week, with straight faces, they ran from side to side, sparks flying all around, not only thrilling this impressionable young boy, but also leaving him a lifelong fascination with submarines and the sea.

CONTENTS

CRADLE OF THE DEEP

Captain David Bannon slipped off his cap and hung it carelessly on the nearest length of pipework. He scrubbed at his slicked-back, wavy red hair. "Up periscope." Leaning on the scope's handles he performed a quick three-sixty degree scan of the outside. The sea was calm and clear. "Steering: what's our position?"

"Currently three nautical miles out of Norfolk, sir, heading due east."

"Very well. Down 'scope." Bannon winked at his young second-in-command, Commander Brad Munrow, who was standing close by, before casting an eye over the handful of picked men manning the control room. They all looked nervously eager. "Gentlemen, on this March 23rd, 1936, the US Navy is about to make history. Welcome to the shakedown cruise of the *USS SC-1*: the world's biggest and ugliest sardine can. I trust you all appreciate what an honour and a privilege it is for you to be here."

"Swell," said one of the steersmen: a fresh-faced blond sailor who didn't look old enough for the job. "But I'd rather be living in Philadelphia." There was a soft, appreciative round of laughter.

"Okay, stow it, Slade" commented Munrow, though he was smiling himself. Bannon knew the feeling: first trip around the bay in a brand new boat with barely dry paintwork. Plenty of room for a screw-up.

Bannon checked his wristwatch. "Secure for dive."

"Secure for dive, aye sir."

"Sound diving stations."

"Diving stations, aye sir." A klaxon blared twice.

Munrow picked up a clipboard and stopwatch. "Ready to dive, Captain."

"Very well. Let's see what this baby can do."

"Aye, sir. Diving control: dive, dive, dive!"

Bannon felt the slight shift under his feet as the sub's bows dipped fractionally. "Level off at periscope depth."

"Periscope depth, aye sir."

Bannon heard the faint metallic ring of waves closing around the boat's hull. His experienced ears also caught the distant grumble of plates accustoming themselves to the weight of water.

"Periscope depth, Captain."

"Very well. Up 'scope." Bannon performed another three-sixty: the ocean remained clear of observers. He pulled a cigar from a shirt pocket and jammed it between his teeth. "Down 'scope. Steady as she goes. Take her down to two hundred feet."

"Two hundred feet, steady as she goes, aye sir."

The distant groans grew louder as the pressure on the boat's outer hull increased. Bannon always found the sound relaxing: like the creak of rigging on the schooners he'd done his early training on. He could also pick out the hum of the twin electric engines: a distant vibration travelling along the hull.

He frowned. Was that vibration just a little too loud? Engines were unique: no two sounded exactly alike, so maybe he was just jittery. Even so, he murmured to Munrow.

"Make a note, Brad: possible engine imbalance." Something for the grease monkeys back at Norfolk to look into a little fine tuning. The commander nodded, checked his stopwatch and scribbled on the clipboard.

"Two hundred feet, Captain," announced diving.

"Very well. All stations, report."

Each station sounded off: diving, steering, ballast control. No one reported any problems. The boat was behaving just fine. Bannon called up the engine room on the talker phone: everything back there was also running sweetly.

He glanced Munrow's way. "What do you say we take her down to test depth?"

The commander returned an easy grin. "Guess that's what we're out here for."

Bannon slapped his arm. "Make it three hundred fifty feet!"

"Three hundred and fifty feet, aye sir."

The boat descended. Bannon watched the depth gauge, its needle slowly counting off the feet of water above them. The hull muttered a couple more times in token protest. The crew were silent: wrapped in their own tasks.

"Three hundred and fifty feet."

"Very well. Level off. Anyone have any bad news?"

Each station snapped back a verbal confirmation: no problems.

"Very well," said Bannon. "Steady as she goes."

"Steady as she goes, aye sir."

"And diving: take us down another hundred feet."

"Four hundred and fifty?" murmured Munrow. "You sure, Captain? That's pretty close to design depth."

"The boys back home assured me the boat should be good to six hundred."

"Should?" Munrow's face was wry. "All due respect to the guys in white coats, Captain, but they're not the ones risking wet feet."

Bannon chuckled. "You worry too much, Brad. Diving?"

"Four hundred fifty feet – aye sir."

There was a period of tense silence. Eyes surreptitiously glanced at the depth gauge. Eventually the sub reached the requested depth. No leaks, no terminal groans. No one had any grief to report.

Bannon glanced at Munrow. The younger man's eyes twinkled with relief. "Make a note, Mr Munrow: test depth safely passed by one hundred feet. That ought to keep the brass happy. Take us back to three fifty."

Munrow scribbled on the clipboard. "As you say—"

There was a loud, dragging sound from outside: like something big was rubbing itself against the hull. Bannon felt the boat yaw.

Munrow steadied himself. "What in hell...?"

"Up 'scope!" Bannon grabbed the periscope handles. There was another dragging noise. Bannon clearly heard it moving from bow to stern. This time the sub shuddered. The captain, face pressed against the eyepiece, scanned the ocean through the periscope.

"Anything?" he heard Munrow asking.

Outside was a deep, uniform blue. Bannon glimpsed the twin gun barrels forward of the conning tower, the deck abaft. "Not that I..." His voice tailed off, mouth suddenly dry. "Son of a—!"

The sub lurched, going down by the stern. Bannon clung onto the scope for support.

"We're fouled!" Munrow called.

"Down 'scope! Blow main ballast!" Bannon glanced at his second-in-command, mind still reeling. "So much for a cosy trip round the bay!"

"Captain!" called diving. "We're not rising. The boat's held fast."

"What in hell's out there?" Munrow muttered.

Bannon ignored him, not ready to answer. But being so close to design depth suddenly didn't seem such a swell idea. He called up the engine room. "Chief. Open her up. Give her everything you've got!"

"*Aye, sir.*"

The sounds of the engines thrummed round the hull, increasing in pitch. Several thuds echoed through the interior. The sub's bow rose, but Bannon didn't need diving control's report to know the boat wasn't moving.

"Emergency main ballast tank blow!" he ordered. "Everyone hold on tight!"

The boat groaned. Bannon heard the roar as every last drop of water was blown out of the tanks with high pressure air. The floor reared. For a while it didn't look like it had made any difference: the boat was still held fast. Then, with a surge, the *SC-1* came free. The pressure gauge dropped with alarming speed.

"Adjust your trim!" yelled Bannon. "We don't want to fly out the water!"

The sub's angle flattened until it was rising almost level. The captain didn't need gauges to know when the sub broke the surface: for a moment he felt weightless as the boat broached like a playful whale, before settling back into the sea.

"Everyone okay?" he called. There was a chorus of assent. "Up 'scope!"

Bannon stared hard. Even blurred by seawater running down the lens, the stern was clearly fouled. By something. Something that had come up with the boat. Something still moving.

He stepped back. "Take a look, Brad. Tell me I'm not going crazy."

Munrow peered through the periscope. He stiffened, turning to stare at his commanding officer. "Better make that two of us," he murmured.

CS૪O

Leigh Oswin let the New York *Times* she was reading droop. Over it, she watched Damian Paladin lounging across a sofa, bare feet hanging off its padded arm. He was half-dressed, black hair sticking up in a Stan Laurel shock, frowning at a copy of *Colliers* magazine.

"You read about that Lane DiRoca bird?" she asked, brushing at a stray lock of her blonde hair and searching for her cigarettes.

He glanced up. "Huh?"

"He's making quite a splash on the West Coast." She lit up. "Least, his alias is." She quoted from the last few inches of column newsprint. "Santa Barbara. Thursday. The mysterious figure known as the Black Tarot is believed to have struck again. Yesterday, local businessman and assistant to the DA's Office, Feldman Nordstrop, was handed over to the authorities along with a dossier itemising his criminal activities. Long suspected of having gangland connections, Nordstrop has evaded arrest up until now, but the damning evidence – presented, according to a precinct desk sergeant, by a masked figure in a long black cape, who vanished with the wave of a playing card – is conclusive enough for an easy conviction."

She dropped the paper again. "Remember when you used to get write-ups like that?"

Damy half-shook his head. "Small time crooks? Is that what he's wasting his time on? He should try facing down four tons of pissed *krovotecheniye zuba* first thing in the morning. Before coffee."

"Yeah, yeah. You're a real *bogatyr*." She allowed the *Times* to slide to the carpet. "We need to get you back in Joe Public's eye again, Damy. Private jobs for émigré Russians doesn't make the papers. Takings at the *Palace* have dived since Christmas: you're becoming yesterday's news."

"Cleaning the DA's Office of wise guys won't make me any friends." He returned his attention to his magazine. "Besides, there'd be nobody left."

"Cynic." She reclined deeply into her chair, blowing smoke rings toward the ceiling. "I just need an angle—"

A knock on the apartment door interrupted her. Damy covered his face with the magazine.

"I'll get it, shall I?" Leigh swept to her feet, a moment later swinging wide the door. Jimmy, the Teton Building's youngest concierge, was on the other side, already blushing.

"Why, good morning!" Leigh angled herself against the doorframe with all the allure she could muster.

Jimmy's eyes bugged. He cleared his throat twice. "Miss Oswin. You have a visitor. Well, Mr Paladin does."

Leigh took a pull on her cigarette. "Really?"

A grizzled, red-haired hunk in US Navy khaki stepped into view, tucking his cap under an arm.

"Captain David Bannon, ma'am. Is Mr Paladin in?"

Leigh allowed her eyes to linger on the Navy man for a couple more seconds. She'd let the *ma'am* go this time. "Damy!" She raised her voice a little. "Get your pants on, hero. You're being pressganged."

෬৪৩

Dressed more properly and sipping lousy coffee which Jimmy had rustled up from someplace, Paladin listened as Captain Bannon rambled on about everything except the reason he was here. Leigh appeared to be hanging on his every pointless word, though. Maybe it was the uniform. He was a big guy, and it fit in all the right places.

Eventually losing patience, Paladin put down his barely-touched coffee and interrupted the Navy man's ramble. "Let's can the small talk. You're not here to debate the weather."

"Don't be rude, Damy," commented Leigh.

Bannon shook his head. "No – he's right, Miss Oswin. I should get to the point." The captain fidgeted with his cap, clearly ill at ease. He cleared his throat. "I believe Admiral Standley considers you a discreet man."

"That's big of him."

Bannon cleared his throat again. "This is all in the strictest confidence." He glanced Leigh's way. "That is clearly understood?"

"I'm deaf, dumb and blind, admiral," grinned Leigh. "You can talk."

Bannon nodded. "Very well. It's not a widely known fact, but the Navy recently launched a new submarine – the *USS SC-1*."

Leigh reached into her purse and produced a pack of cigarettes. "Secret submarine. Gotcha." She offered the captain a smoke.

He accepted, lighting it and her own. "It's the biggest sub in the world: four hundred feet. Larger than the French cruiser sub, *Surcouf*."

Paladin shrugged. "Means nothing to me."

"Of course." Bannon took a deep drag on his cigarette. "Submarines are the future of naval warfare, Paladin, the Great War showed us that. Both the British and French are investing in huge boats – submarine cruisers – armed with large deck guns alongside conventional torpedoes, and onboard airplane hangars."

"And the US Navy wants bigger toys."

"By forty feet or more. The *SC-1* has no hangar, but it is armed with a twin barrelled, eight inch turret gun. It can also dive in excess of three hundred feet, travel at around twenty five knots on the surface, and just under twenty, submerged."

"Is that good?" Leigh enquired.

"It's faster and deeper than any boat in operation."

Paladin scratched his cheek. "Okay, I doubt you're here just to brag about the Navy's newest underwater doodad. Level with me."

Bannon's cap was spinning faster than a phonograph record. "The sub recently performed its first shakedown run. It descended past its test depth. It didn't come back alone."

"There, that wasn't so hard." Paladin relaxed in his chair. "So what did it drag up? The ghost of Moby Dick?"

"It—" Bannon sighed in something like frustration. "I don't know what it is!"

Leigh chuckled. "Your boys caught a mermaid? Nifty!"

Paladin was thoughtful. "Usually the other way round, princess. You said 'is', Captain. That mean it's still alive?"

Bannon looked like he was about to admit to something really dirty. "Yes. Back in Norfolk they hauled it off the sub and dumped it in a cistern."

Paladin and Leigh exchanged glances. "And you want me to go take a look at it," he said.

"Some people thought it might be a good idea."

"Like the Chief of Naval Operations, maybe?"

The captain gave a reluctant nod, half smiling. "And my second-in-command is a quite the follower of your exploits. So he—"

"Hear that, princess? I have a follower." Paladin grinned at her pained expression. "You wanted an angle: we got a mermaid to look at!"

Leigh mashed out her cigarette. "Swell. I'll go get my swimsuit."

∞

Outside it was grey and drizzling. There was a pennant-sporting limo waiting out on Central Park West. Decked out in their signature flying jackets and gun belts, Leigh and Paladin slid into the wide rear seat as Bannon sat himself next to a female Yeoman driver. She guided the limo into traffic once everyone was settled.

They drove to a Naval Reserve base out on Long Island. A few planes stood on its runway, one of them a yellow and silver Lockheed Orion passenger plane in USN markings. The driver pulled up right alongside it. Bannon opened the limo's passenger door, gesturing for Leigh and Paladin to climb aboard. Obviously they weren't going to get a grand tour of the base.

Inside the plane was pretty ritzy: seats for six passengers, in pale, padded leather. The walls matched. Paladin dropped into a seat right at the front – the one nearest the door had a valise on it – stroking the thick armrest.

"You do well for yourself, Captain."

Bannon shrugged. "You're getting the works, Paladin. Normally only Admirals and above get this kind of ride."

Leigh took the seat across the narrow aisle from Paladin. "I could get used to it." She stretched out her booted legs and sighed. "Our tax dollars at work."

A moment later, the Orion's engine roared to life. The pilot wasn't wasting any time. Before it even started taxiing, Bannon had hooked up the valise and moved to the back of the small cabin.

The airplane's single engine grew louder. It accelerated, bouncing across the airstrip, quickly lifting into the air. Paladin looked out his window: the Reserve Base was already below and behind them. The plane banked, changing course. They were heading slightly west of due south: straight for Norfolk, Paladin figured. Low cloud swirled around the climbing Orion, and the land vanished. A minute later they emerged into sunlight. The sky was a pale, steel blue, clots of white cloud reared all around like vast banks of raw cotton.

It was a short flight. In what felt like no time the plane was on the ground, taxiing towards a group of low buildings. Beyond reared tall shipyard derricks. It wasn't raining, but the sky was still leaden and threatening.

They followed Bannon across a damp landing strip towards another Navy limo that was the twin of the one they'd left in New York. There was a twin female Yeoman at the wheel, too. If it wasn't for the changed horizon, Paladin could have believed they'd just circled back to Long Island.

They were driven straight to the Naval shipyards. Paladin received an impression of acres of docks and wharves, derricks and steam cranes running on rail tracks, endless numbers of single floor buildings, but not many ships. There were a handful of small vessels – a couple in dry dock – that were either being repaired or refitted. Even then, there wasn't much activity.

"Where are all the battleships?" he wondered out loud.

"Where they belong," was Bannon's only comment.

Finally they pulled down a long wharf. On the seaward side was a moored vessel, but no boarding ramps in view. A line of low brick buildings ran along the wharf as far as the sea. Offices or warehouses of some kind, Paladin figured.

Bannon opened the right passenger door, allowing Leigh out. Paladin opened his own door and stood looking up at the moored vessel. At first he thought it was a corvette or similar: a huge turret sat amidships, and there were machine guns mounted at various points. Then he realised just how streamlined the turret and superstructure behind it was. Like it had been designed by a Modernist painter.

"That's the sub?" He hadn't imagined just how big it might be.

The driver blocked his way, hands negligently behind her back. Even though she stood a good foot shorter than him, Paladin guessed she'd be no pushover. She raised an arm, hand gesturing towards the line of buildings.

"This way, sir."

"Thank you, Yeoman." He tried out his grin. It didn't work.

It wasn't hard to guess where whatever had come up with the sub was stored. Two sailors in crackerjack suits stood guard by one door, rifles grounded. Paladin caught up with Leigh and Bannon. The guards snapped to attention, saluting the approaching captain. Bannon stood aside for Paladin and Leigh to pass through.

Inside was lit by ranks of naked lightbulbs. The space wasn't large: bricked off either side of the door to create a space around thirty feet long. There were two windows in both front and back walls. The floor was cut away: what remained was not much more than a railed off balcony overlooking a deep, dark space. An officer in khaki was staring down at the void, negligently leaning on the railing. A couple of sailors in dungarees hung about by the far wall. The officer straightened up and turned a wide smile on the approaching trio.

Leigh almost purred. "Who's Joel McCrea?"

"Commander Brad Munrow," said Bannon. He seemed more relaxed: back on familiar turf. "The sub's second-in-command."

The commander saluted, the smile never leaving his lips. "So I finally get to meet the famous monster hunter. I've read a lot about you, Mr Paladin."

Paladin shook his hand. "You should hear what the papers don't print."

Munrow removed his cap, revealing neatly clipped black hair. "While you must be Miss Oswin."

"Must I?" Leigh smiled mischievously. "If you insist."

Bannon joined Munrow at the rail. "Any change?"

The commander shrugged. "It hasn't budged since you left for New York. Water's swirled a couple of times, but otherwise..."

Paladin stared down. The void was a brick-lined pit with steel ladders at every corner. It was filled with dark water, rising to some ten feet below floor level. A strong fishy odour thickened the air. It wasn't the kind of pool he'd ever want to take a dip in. "So what we got?"

"This cistern can be filled with seawater," said Munrow. He pulled a battered pack of cigarettes from a shirt pocket and offered them around. Bannon and Leigh each took one and lit up. "A dozen of us managed to drag and dump what we brought up into there. It fought every inch of the way. No one was seriously hurt, just some bruises, a few stings or burns." He blew a billow of smoke towards the water's surface. "I think we got lucky."

Paladin frowned. "And it's done nothing since?"

"It thrashed about at first – beating at the water and the sides. After a time it quietened. Maybe it's dying. Or dead."

Paladin stared down at the black water. He shivered.

"You want to take a look?" asked Bannon.

"It's why I'm here. Long as I don't have to climb down."

The captain shook his head. "Not necessary." He raised his voice. "Drain it!"

One of the sailors threw a switch and the whine of pumps filled the room. The water level began to drop. Paladin watched the surface as it swirled: disturbed by the pumps, or something else.

A moment later the seawater erupted: a cold geyser. Something long and thick spewed upwards, reaching higher than the railings. Paladin and the two officers gave way, already half soaked. Paladin's hand reached for his Mauser 9mm.

The thing rearing above the rail was like a smooth, vast, translucent snake, almost six feet at its thickest. Where its head should have been was a crude sphere, covered in tendrils which writhed, stretched, and withdrew.

"Fall back!" ordered Bannon, somewhat unnecessarily.

The drone of the pumps was punctuated by gunfire: one of the sailors had taken up a rifle and was plugging away at the weaving shape. All the shells seemed to be doing was irritating the thing. It twitched, turning, the tendril covered end bobbing like a cobra.

"Sailor!" yelled Bannon. "I said fall back!"

The spherical tip struck. The sailor was enveloped by the writhing, stabbing tendrils. His scream was mercifully short. The huge shape bent double, arcing towards the dropping water level, taking the enveloped body.

Paladin leapt to the railing. He squeezed the Mauser's trigger. Twenty slugs ripped through the coiling shape in a second. Chunks of gelatinous flesh spun off. It didn't seem to care. At Paladin's side, Leigh calmly drew her Luger and plugged away, with no more effect than shooting a sack full of Jell-O.

Most of the water had drained away. The shape, the sailor's body bundled at one end, was pushing against the cistern's floor, like it was trying to force the corpse through the brickwork.

"Reflex action." Paladin holstered his gun. The sailor was beyond help now.

"Reflex?" Bannon stared at him.

"Feeding. It's trying to drop prey into a mouth that's no longer there."

Below, the floor was filled with thick, heaving, translucent coils. Paladin yanked four incendiary grenades from pouches on his modified cartridge belt, juggling two in each hand. He yanked the first two pins with his teeth, dropping the grenades on the writhing coils. Pulling the second pair of pins, he sent the incendiaries to join the first.

"Everybody get the hell back!"

He ran for the front wall, hoping Leigh and the Navy men would take the hint. Seconds later there was a flash which seared the back of Paladin's eyeballs. A white hot balloon grew out of the cistern. He could hear water boiling away into steam. The stench of burning flooded the room.

Once he'd blinked away the after-image, Paladin edged his way back to the cistern and looked down. The floor was still burning, the brick sides smoking and steaming. A charred, half-melted mess was all that remained of the coils.

Bannon joined him, swearing under his breath. "What the hell?"

"Phosphorous. Sorry – it was the first thing I thought of."

Leigh leaned over the railing. She whistled softly. "Some bell bottom's got plenty of scrubbing to do."

൭൭

Sitting in a warm office next to a banked fire, all four waited as their seawater shower dried off. They hugged mugs of coffee. Everyone but Paladin smoked.

"Well, I guess you got rid of it," Bannon was saying. "Shame about the damage to Navy property."

Leigh chuckled. "That's his trademark."

"I didn't get rid of it." Paladin stared at the fire, thinking hard. "Not completely."

"Sure." Bannon leaned forward. "You said something about it feeding a mouth that wasn't there."

"What's *that* mean?" asked Commander Munrow. He looked intrigued, eager.

"You've seen sea anemones, corals – that kind of thing. You know how they feed."

Munrow nodded. "They catch prey in tentacles, which usually contain stinging cells. The stunned prey is then fed into the mouth around— Hey, are you suggesting that was part of a sea anemone?" The idea seemed to excite him.

"That would be crazy." Paladin shook his head, amused at the commander's eagerness. "But it was a feeder arm, all right. A damned big one. The stinging tentacles were all concentrated in that lump at the tip."

"That's fantastic!"

"I'm sure the sailor who died thought so too, Brad," murmured Bannon.

Munrow dropped his gaze. "Yes. I'm sorry, Captain,"

Bannon threw his cigarette into the fire. "Paladin, you're telling me that out in the Atlantic is a whale-sized invertebrate that catches subs for breakfast?"

"I guess."

Leigh drained her coffee. "So – what do we do, my *bogatyr*?"

Paladin got to his feet. "Persuade it to amscray, if I can. Captain: I need to go back to New York for a few items. May we borrow your plane? Leigh can fly it."

Bannon looked tired, defeated. "Sure. Why not? I'll have you driven back to the airfield."

"And while we're away, have a word with my old friend Admiral Standley. I need to borrow the world's biggest submarine."

⊗⊗⊗

When Paladin stepped down into the control room, his first thought was how spacious the interior of the *SG-1* was. Sure, it was a pipe-fitter's nightmare: a maze of tubes and dials, wheels and stopcocks of one kind or another, covering the curve of the inner hull. The designer hadn't missed a gap that couldn't be crammed with a couple more instruments. But it wasn't anything like as cramped as he'd imagined. Maybe he wouldn't have to take up claustrophobia as a side line after all.

It was hot, though, and smelly. A blend of diesel fuel, oil, metal and ozone. At least there wasn't the rank odour of sweat. That probably moved in after weeks at sea. He really hoped it wouldn't come to that.

Leigh dropped to the floor, followed by Commander Munrow. Captain Bannon stood by the periscope, leaning negligently on a handle. He tipped his cap by way of acknowledgement.

"Welcome aboard, Miss Oswin. And you certainly have some pull with the Chief of Naval Operations, Paladin. Admiral Standley was more than happy for us to take you for a joy ride. He trust you that much?"

"Maybe he just wants to silence me forever."

Bannon winced. "I'll do my best to see that doesn't happen. You get everything you need back in New York?"

"Let's hope so, Captain." Paladin held up two modified cartridge belts, similar to the one cinched around his waist, save for the twin holsters.

Bannon switched his attention to Munrow. "Everything clear topside, Brad?"

"Aye, Captain. Ready to shove off at your word."

"Very well. Excuse me, folks, duty calls." He stepped onto the ladder and climbed out of sight.

"Where's he going?" asked Leigh.

"Bridge," said Munrow. "While the boat's on the surface, there's always someone up top. The captain likes to take manoeuvring watch when we leave and arrive at port."

Leigh looked around the control room. "Guess you guys are pretty blind down here."

There was an electronic crackle: a radio clearing its throat. "Excuse me." Munrow switched on the intercom. "Captain?"

"Lines are cast off. Back us out, Commander."

"Aye, sir." Munrow raised his voice. "Steering: full astern."

"Full astern, aye."

Paladin felt a growing pulse through his feet: the engines waking. There was a faint nudge as the sub backed out of dock. Paladin grabbed at a nearby pipe to steady himself. Leigh did the same.

Bannon's voice came over the intercom at intervals, ordering changes in course. Each time Munrow and the helmsman repeated the order as acknowledgement. Finally they were in open water. Bannon gave a course and ordered full ahead.

Munrow visibly relaxed, his grin returning. "Leaving and entering harbour – not my favourite part."

"Now he tells us," muttered Leigh.

The commander shrugged. "Imagine taking a swim through sharp rocks with your eyes shut." He produced cigarettes and offered them.

Leigh took one with obvious relief. "You can smoke down here?"

"Sure, while we're on the surface." He lit her cigarette.

"When do we dive?" asked Paladin

"The boat needs to clear the continental shelf – around three nautical miles. So—" he glanced at his wristwatch "—just under ten minutes."

"Impressive." Paladin glanced around. "The ship's interior is larger than I'd imagined."

"Boat," Munrow corrected. "And sure: biggest in the world. No matter which way you look at it. Submerged it displaces a little under five thousand tons. When she's commissioned she'll have a full complement of eight officers and one hundred men." He was obviously real proud of the sub. "We actually have two decks – which is kind of unusual."

"That where everybody sleeps?" asked Leigh.

"No – mostly storage. We need someplace to stow spare batteries, and the torpedoes and shells for the deck gun." He smiled easily, dismissive. Obviously that extra deck was used for more than just spare ordnance. "On the surface the boat's powered by twin diesel engines, submerged we use battery power. We run slower under water – but it's a close thing."

Leigh was staring around the control room. "So how do you steer it?"

Munrow pointed forward. "Steering's over there. Works the same as any surface ship." Two crewmen, one a blond kid, the other a burly chestnut, sat at twin wheels. "And over there—" Munrow nodded at a standing crewman "—is diving control. That takes us down and – more important – brings us back up again."

"Not a guy to fall out with."

"You got that right."

The intercom crackled. *"This is manoeuvring watch. Stand by for diving stations."*

"Standing by, Captain."

"Coming down."

"Ready when you are." Munrow pointed at a metal bowl fixed to the wall. "Time to douse that ciggy, Miss Oswin."

As she crushed her smoke out, the captain's feet appeared on the ladder. Bannon paused to seal the hatch before hopping lightly to the floor.

"Up 'scope." Bannon peered through the eyepieces, slowly turning it through three hundred and sixty degrees. "Diving stations. Take her down, Brad. Periscope depth." He slipped a cold cigar into his mouth.

Munrow smiled briefly at both Paladin and Leigh. "Hold on folks: this is better than Coney Island. Dive! Dive! Dive!"

Paladin felt the deck tilt. From outside came a muted, oddly metallic sound. He felt cold – but that was likely imagination.

Bannon checked through the periscope one last time. "Down 'scope. Steering: maintain course at due east. Diving: take us down to two hundred feet."

Both stations acknowledged the order. Bannon stepped away from the periscope and joined Munrow, Leigh and Paladin. "How are you enjoying the dive?" he asked.

Leigh was staring up at the control room roof. "Does it always creak like that?"

"Just the outer hull," said Munrow. "The increasing weight of the water. Sounds worse than it is."

"You sure?"

"Relax, Miss Oswin," said the captain. "We got safety margins, and then some."

She didn't look mollified. "Relax, he says!"

Bannon unrolled a chart across a small waist-high table next to the periscope. There was a large *X* marked on it. The captain tapped it with his cigar. "This is where we were so rudely interrupted."

Paladin leaned closer. "What's our position now?"

Munrow indicated a point west of the mark.

"And how deep were you when it struck?"

Captain and commander exchanged glances. "Four hundred fifty feet," Bannon finally admitted.

Paladin whistled. A thought occurred to him. "How do you intend to find whatever's out there? I assume you won't be looking through that periscope all the time."

The officers swapped looks again. "The boat has an experimental system on board," Munrow explained. "Sound location. We send out a ping and listen for echoes."

Paladin got it. "Like British ships used to locate U-boats in the war, using hydrophones"

Munrow nodded. "Kind of. The Navy's been testing various systems since the Twenties. This is the latest version. It's pretty powerful, I'm told."

"So why didn't it detect our sea monster before?"

"I wish you wouldn't call it that." The captain looked pained. "Like Brad says, the system's experimental. We were taking the *SG-1* out for a test dive. Trials of the on-board equipment don't begin until the boat's commissioned."

Paladin was getting the strongest impression that the sub wasn't only the first of its class: it was destined to be a floating test-bed as well.

"Captain!" It was the blond-haired kid. "We're in position."

"Very well." Bannon glanced at Paladin. "We've reached the buried treasure." Louder, he ordered, "All stop. Begin descent to four hundred feet, holding every fifty feet. Switch on echo location."

"Beginning descent, Captain. EL enabled."

"Very well." His smiled faltered. "If there's something out there, let's hope the new gear spots it first."

Leigh pursed her lips. "And if not?"

Bannon slipped the stogie between his teeth and chewed it. "Then the lab boys are going to get a real terse memo. Excuse me." He joined his sparse crew, watching the depth gauge, staring over the shoulder of another crewman in headphones who was, Paladin guessed by the way he stared at a screen, overseeing the echo location monitor.

All around the control room every face had the same tense look. This wasn't a simple test dive anymore: they were dropping towards something outside their experience. They had every right to be shaky. Paladin's own nerves were quivering, just a little.

He glanced towards Leigh. "Okay, princess?"

"I guess."

"Wishing you hadn't come?"

Her answering grin was feral. "You know better than that!"

"Two hundred fifty feet!"

Bannon acknowledged the call. "Very well. Proceed."

The faint groans from outside punctuated a silence that grew thicker with every passing moment. With the engines shut off, the sub itself was eerily quiet.

"Three hundred feet!"

"Very well. Anything on EL?"

"Nothing, Captain."

"Very well. Proceed."

Paladin felt the beginnings of a headache. He rubbed the back of his neck. How in hell did these guys stand it? Prowling the seas without so much as a porthole to look out of. From now on he'd stick to airplanes.

"Three hundred fifty feet!"

"EL clear."

"Very well. Proceed."

"Contact, Captain!"

"Diving: hold position!" Bannon leaned closer to the screen. "Where away?"

"Ten degrees off the port bow, around ninety feet below the keel."

"Is it moving?"

"No, sir. Maintaining position."

"Very well. Steering: back us off gently. Maintain depth." The captain looked towards Paladin and Leigh. "Our bogeyman?"

The background hum of reawakened engines filled the silence. "Could be," agreed Paladin.

Bannon returned his attention to the EL operator. "The contact still on screen?"

"Aye, Captain. Holding position."

"Stop engines. Diving: proceed to four hundred feet. EL: if that contact so much as twitches in our direction, sing out."

"Aye, Captain."

"What now?" Paladin wondered out loud.

Commander Munrow answered. "I guess we try sneaking up on it. At four hundred feet it'll still be another forty or so below us."

"And then?" asked Leigh.

Paladin winked at her. "Then I go for a swim."

"Four hundred feet!"

"Level off," ordered the captain. "EL, how's that contact?"

"Still holding position, Captain."

"Very well." Bannon straightened and addressed the crew. "Gentlemen – and lady – this is where the fun starts. I want us to move in as close as possible to whatever's out there. Slow and gentle so's not to provoke it." He stared down at the EL screen again. "Steering: take us forward, minimum revs."

"Minimum revs, aye sir."

Leigh stared up at Paladin. She looked twitchy. Raging inside at not being able to get involved. Take control of her own destiny. But they were guests on board a submarine that was most likely top secret. Neither of them had any authority, and Admiral Standley's influence was a long way away.

The captain's voice overrode anything Paladin might have said. "How far to the contact?"

"Around one hundred feet, Captain. Stationary— No, belay that! It's rising! Coming straight up—!"

Bannon rushed to the EL screen. "Full astern! Get us out of here!" A moment later the submarine lurched to port. What sounded like the world's biggest baseball bat pounded on the hull. Leigh was flung halfway across the control room. Paladin found himself up against a maze of pipework. He hung on tight. The sub tipped to starboard. Officers and crew were tossed like dolls.

Bannon threw himself against the periscope housing, snatching for the handles. "Steering: I gave you an order!"

"Full astern, aye sir!"

Paladin felt the rising vibration as the engines spun up to full power. Leigh grabbed the small table, pulling herself to her feet.

Bannon was checking through the periscope, muttering under his breath. Fighting against the pitching floor, Munrow joined him. "We fouled again?"

Bannon drew back and shook his head. "Don't see anything. Must be under the keel. What's on EL?" he called.

"Contact dropping away, Captain."

The sub had steadied. Crewmen got back on their feet, clutching bruised and battered limbs. Everyone was bleeding, some badly.

Paladin relaxed his grip and began unbuttoning his flying coat. "Looks like I'm up."

⋘⋙

Paladin looked at the thing dangling from his hand with a certain degree of trepidation. "And I can breathe through this?" He'd been expecting something more like the metal-helmeted, Frankenstein monster booted diving suit. Not the vulcanised cloth get-up Commander Munrow had helped him into.

They were close to the boat's bow in a small, spartan compartment just forward of the deck-to-keel cylinder which was the eight inch deck gun's mount and magazine. From a row of hooks hung rubbery suits like the one Paladin wore. Another wall was stacked with compressed air cylinders. Behind him was a simple door leading to an airlock and the escape hatch. The whole place was lit by one dim bulkhead lamp.

Munrow took the mess of straps and tubes from Paladin and held it up. "The whole thing fits snugly over your head, including the clear faceplate. A little water will get in – that's to be expected. This part covers your mouth and nose – again, it might leak a tad – and you breathe normally. Air comes from this." He tapped the compressed air tank strapped to Paladin's chest by a metal and webbing harness. "It employs a regulator and non-return valve, based on a design by a French guy. Le Prieur."

Paladin took the mask back. "Don't tell me – it's experimental."

Munrow chuckled. "Worked fine in that big cistern back in Norfolk."

"That's a comfort."

34

"There's enough air for a ten minute dive at this depth." Munrow tapped a small gauge on top of the cylinder. "But you wouldn't want to be out much longer, anyhow."

"Why's that?"

"Caisson disease – decompression sickness. The longer you stay out, the worse it gets."

"And if I'm out longer than ten minutes?"

"There's a hyperbaric chamber on board. We can decompress you before too much damage is done." Munrow was smiling again. Paladin couldn't tell if he was kidding around or being comforting. Not that it mattered. If anyone on board could ride out the effects of deep water, it was Paladin.

He paused halfway to fitting the mask on. "You might want to find something to occupy Leigh. Until I get back, she's likely to be like a bearcat with two sore heads."

The commander laughed shortly. "With half this token crew laid up, we could use all the help we can get." He thought a moment. "How is she with a wheel?"

"She drives like she's flying, and flies like a 500-mile race car driver. If you need to get someplace in a hurry, she's your gal."

"Good enough. Johnny Slade busted an arm, she can take his position on steering." Munrow squeezed Paladin's shoulder, his eyes concerned. "You okay with this? There's going to be close on two hundred pounds per square inch pressure out there. I heard you've come through some crazy stuff, but—"

"Kind of late to be worrying, isn't it?" Paladin hitched the two cartridge belts around his waist into a more comfortable position. "I'm your best bet for dealing with what's out there. Besides, the ocean and me have an understanding. Ask Leigh."

He pulled the mask over his face. It smelled funny. Munrow helped him tighten the four straps around the back of his head. Once the commander was done, Paladin felt like his face was being crushed by a rubber octopus.

Munrow stepped in front. "All set?"

Paladin raised a thumb, glad he couldn't talk clearly. He felt far from okay. Munrow made a couple more adjustments to the air cylinder and suddenly Paladin could breathe better. He made the thumbs up gesture again.

"One more thing. It's not totally dark out there, but it's still around one percent of sunlight at the surface. The water will look the same shade of blue all over, and it's easy to get disorientated. Perspective gets screwed." Munrow held up a coil of what looked like grey rope. "This is woven from chrome-steel wire. It'll hold an elephant. Once you're outside, snap this clip onto the forward deck rail." He dropped the coil into Paladin's hand, at the same time securing the other end to his harness with a carabiner.

Munrow spun the wheel on the airlock door and opened it. "Once you're locked in I'll flood the compartment. The water's going to come in slow, but it'll be at pressure. It'll sting. Try not to panic. Just breathe normally."

Paladin flapped into the airlock, finding it hard to walk in the swim fins on his feet. Inside he turned to face Munrow. The commander was already closing and locking the door. It went very dark, very quickly.

Why would I panic? he wondered. A moment later frigid water began pouring invisibly in. Paladin gasped at the shrivelling cold. *I had to ask.*

Within a minute he was engulfed. He felt his body being squeezed. For an instant a sharp pain lanced through his ears into his brain. He was half deafened by the roar of the water – then everything fell quiet. All he heard was the rattle of his breathing in the air tube, expired bubbles gurgling past his ears. He pushed off the floor, reaching for the overhead hatch. Undogging it he rose up, almost braining himself on a second, external hatch.

Unlocked, it swung up and away. Paladin pulled himself out into the open ocean.

For a moment, he was frozen by what he saw. In all directions the water was a uniform violet. He felt like he could reach out and touch it. The gun turret reared over him, clear against the backdrop, tinted blue. Remembering to clip his cable onto the deck rail, Paladin swum above the turret. He could see the boat's hull laid out before him. Blue-grey against the unchanging backdrop, attenuated light beams rippling over its surface, it was his only reference point, his only sense of perspective. He understood the commander's words: without the sub's huge presence he'd have no idea of what was up, down, or of distance.

That was the moment he sensed it, looming behind him. He spun awkwardly about. Rising above the sub's bow, like an upended, opalescent zeppelin, was a pale giant of a thing. Its base was hidden by the sub, but its pale top stood out stark against the dark water. Countless huge arms, identical to the thing back in the cistern, waved slowly from the upper end, each terminating in globes of smaller, undulating tendrils. They clutched at the water, nonstop.

It was like a vast sea anemone, held aloft by a broad stalk.

As Paladin floated, a shark swam by, its cold eyes watching curiously. Paladin blew a stream of bubbles, and it shied away, alarmed. The shark brushed against one of the arms, and was instantly enfolded by tendrils. It thrashed a moment, then fell still. The arm folded back on itself, hauling the shark towards the broad top. The animal was plunged whole into a fleshy aperture. After a few moments, the arm slid out. The shark was gone.

The pale mass, arms writhing, gradually descended. Once it was out of sight, Paladin dropped back to the deck and pulled himself forward along the deck rail. Peering cautiously over the sub's prow, he watched as the thing sank into deeper, darker waters. It didn't quite vanish: palely outlined against the purple twilight depths, its huge arms continued to wave gracefully.

Paladin didn't think it would stay there for long. It probably bobbed up and down, all the time feeling for anything unlucky enough to come within reach. On its first encounter, the sub had likely grazed a feeding arm, the second time the thing had come up directly below, hitting the sub's keel and retreating in alarm. Recoiling from something its primitive senses recognised as too big or a potential threat.

It reminded him of something: a huge, corpse-white monstrosity hiding under Seattle. He'd creamed that with sack loads of salt. This bloated slug was living quite happily in seawater, so that wasn't an option.

And just how big was it? How deep was the water out here? He should have checked with Bannon, or Munrow. If that thing was anchored on the bottom, it could be unbelievably tall. And was it fully grown? A growth spurt might see it crest the last four hundred feet. It could pick small ships off the surface like a Venus flytrap snaring bugs.

His hands rested on the modified cartridge belts, toying with the pouches. What did he have that might fry it? It wasn't supernatural, far as he could tell. Even if the sub was carrying torpedoes, he didn't think a couple of exploding fish would have much effect. Mauser and Luger slugs hadn't bothered the detached arm one bit. Likely, torpedoes would just slide through the gelatinous body and come out the other side without detonating. Or could the good captain detonate torpedoes remotely?

He rejected the idea: too close to the sub. They'd sink themselves along with the creature.

It was rising again. Slow, but with the unstoppablity of an express train.

Back in Norfolk, the torn off arm had burned easily enough – but that had been out of water. Phosphorus wasn't going to cut it down here. He'd fetched a bunch of magical offensives from New York, and they were going to be as much help as incendiary grenades. What else did he have...?

The frill of arms rose majestically past the prow. Paladin shrank back. Hand over hand, he retreated along the rail six feet or so. As the pale head of the creature came into view, Paladin realised a loop of his steel anchoring cable was hanging off the sub's bow, almost daring one of the undulating arms to snare it.

He tugged at the cable, reeling it in. It twisted. The loop rolled over in a lazy counter-clockwise arc. Just as it reached the twelve o'clock position, an arm brushed against it.

The nest of tendrils at the arm's tip closed around the cable. The arm began to curl back. A hooked fish, Paladin was hauled after it.

The cable might have held an elephant, it couldn't withstand the weight of a submarine. It snapped, leaving several feet hanging off the deck rail.

Struggling, half-panicked, Paladin snatched at the carabiner clipped to his breathing harness. His cold hands fumbled to release it. The knot of tendrils around the cable was dipping towards the maw. They plunged inside.

The clip snapped open. Paladin dived free.

Pumping his legs, he swam for the sub. Another arm rolled by. Twisting, he somehow avoided it.

And swam straight into another.

Tendrils enclosed him, clamping down tighter than anything so soft and pliable had a right to do. It was like fighting a hundred living ropes. Every attempt he made to jerk free just squeezed him tighter. Somehow he kept his facemask on.

Fire erupted all over his body: it was stinging him. His rubber suit was no barrier to the oversized poisoned barbs. He felt himself go limp, immobilised by pain, or shock. His breathing grew shallow, spasmodic. Numbness swept over him. At least it dulled the pain.

Glimpsed between the tendrils looping past his facemask he saw the sub, apparently above him, the image dancing in and out of vision. Then it dropped abruptly away. For a moment all Paladin saw was the endless violet ocean – then even that was engulfed in blackness. The tendrils' grip slackened. He was left suspended, unable to move, in a lightless void which slowly churned and pressed on all sides.

What a revolting development, he thought, realising where he'd wound up. *I'll never look at oysters the same way again.*

Agony swept through him again from head to toe. His nerves were waking up. He managed to twitch his hands – movement was returning. Painfully. He tried to console himself by thinking no one else on board the sub could have survived those stinging cells. It didn't help.

He fumbled in his belt pouches with uncoordinated fingers, finally closing around the shape he was groping for. He drew it out, twisting the stubby cigar shape in numb hands. The spring-loaded interior clicked. Instantly it was three times longer, more like a baton. The internal single-use battery discharged its voltage in one go, igniting a magnesium flare. Dazzling white light flooded the space.

Was it okay to panic now? He was surrounded by pale, undulating masses of flesh. Above he could just make out the thin slit of the huge thing's mouth – now sealed shut.

In the belly of the beast. Jonah, I take it all back.

With a trembling arm he held the bubbling magnesium torch away from his face: the heat radiating out from it was growing uncomfortable. The surrounding flesh reacted violently, shrinking back from the light, releasing Paladin. He was left floating in a wriggling gullet that was around ten feet across. Coils of the snapped steel cable sank past him. For an experiment, Paladin swam clumsily to one of the sides, pushing his torch right up against it.

The reaction was even more violent. It felt as though the whole creature twitched, shaking Paladin like a cocktail olive.

Giving you heartburn, huh?

He backed off, turning his attention to where the gullet led. A dozen or so feet below, just where the harsh light began to fade, it was pinched shut. He allowed himself to sink, holding the torch at arm's length. Just before he reached the stricture, it sprang open, writhing back from the heat. Another cavern formed, twenty feet or so deep.

He looked back the way he'd come. As expected, now the heat source had gone, the gap was gradually irising shut.

He could probably make it back out: use the torch to force his way up to the mouth, make it disgorge him. But there was still a chance he'd be re-snared before he made it to the sub. Only one thing for it: force his way deeper and ignite all the magnesium flares in one go. With luck, the heat and its own agonies would tear the thing apart,

He pushed on, his body now just an uncoordinated mass of tingles, accompanied by the steel cable. Every time he came close to a wall of flesh, it spasmed wide, opening another pocket. Above him, the sides cautiously closed in again.

His torch began to gutter. Dropping it, he drew out another, extending and igniting it before the light and heat could fade.

Close to where the dying torch had fallen, head and pectoral fins jutting from where its body was pinched inside another gastric wall sphincter, was the dead shark. Paladin drifted close, holding out his fresh torch. The wall belched wide and the shark sank free, gently butting up against the next stricture. Paladin dropped toward it, inspecting the body. There were no signs of digestion yet – in a tract this size, in the cold, he figured that would be a drawn out process.

He waved the torch and the sphincter opened, tumbling the dead shark deeper. The broken cable followed. Paladin had no idea how far he was inside the gigantic thing – maybe sixty to eighty feet – but he was likely still just stuck in what passed for its throat. He wanted to get inside its guts before he unleased hellfire.

He dived deeper, the torch opening his way, the dead shark and steel cable drifting ahead of him every time. At a point he estimated was somewhere around one hundred twenty feet down, he checked his tank's air gauge. There was less than a quarter left. A couple of minutes at most.

Guess this is as good a place as any.

He unbuckled both of the cartridge belts and wrapped them around the shark's body. For good measure, he wound the steel cable about it as well. He was sorry to lose the charms and talismans stored in one belt, but maybe the phosphorus grenades it also held would detonate once the magnesium got going. If it did, there'd be one real unholy explosion down here.

He lit another flare, jamming three spares under his harness. Pushing aside the buckle on the belt containing the flares, his fingers fumbled for a small tab in the leather. Underneath was a wire loop. Paladin hooked a finger through and pulled.

A metal strip came free, unspooling from inside the belt. A few fine bubbles rose as the mixture of sea water and diluted gastric fluids touched the metal contacts inside. The whole belt was now a battery, the chemicals built into it reacting with the water and each other to build a charge. A charge big enough to ignite every magnesium flare simultaneously.

Time I wasn't here.

Holding the torch up front, he pushed away from the twitching floor and swam up fast as his still sluggish muscles let him. He had no idea how long before the battery fired, never tested it. He didn't want to be too close when it did.

The gastric walls peeled back from the torch, never fast enough. It felt like the creature had grown used to the heat, was reacting slower each time. Paladin didn't think he'd ascended more than twenty feet when the pocket he was swimming through contracted violently, crushing him. A second later, the world turned white.

છ๛

Leigh was glad she had the wheel to hang on to. One moment the steersman next to her was explaining how the helm worked, the next it felt like something had grabbed a hold of the sub and was using it like a cocktail shaker. She almost fell backwards out of her chair.

Captain Bannon was hanging off the periscope. "What in hell—?" He hauled himself upright. "EL! How's that contact?"

There was a pause while the operator checked his scope. "Gone, sir."

"Nothing?"

Another pause. Meanwhile the sub righted itself, the crew dusted themselves down and went about like nothing had happened. Leigh wondered if they were getting used to it.

"All clear, Captain."

Bannon grabbed the periscope. He swung around in a circle, scanning every inch of the outside ocean. "Can't see a damned thing! Water's all clouded—!" He froze. "Steering, fifteen degrees left rudder. Half ahead."

Leigh buried her fears, mimicking the steersman at her side. Guiding the sub wasn't like driving a car, or flying a plane.

"All stop." Bannon was still glued to the periscope.

"What is it?" asked Leigh. She was almost too afraid to ask. "Is it Damy?"

"Uh-huh." The captain finally took his eyes off the periscope. He gazed at her with a look she'd seen many times: a confusion of disbelief and delight.

Leigh came out of her seat and grabbed the periscope from Bannon's hands. All she saw was murky blue, like the sea was full of silt. Then a figure, flapping awkwardly, pale against the water. Damy really was a lousy swimmer. She resisted an urge to squeal.

Beside her, she heard Bannon's voice talking into a phone. "Mr Munrow!"

"Captain?"

"Get the hyperbaric chamber warmed up, Brad. Looks like it may have a guest."

ᗰᗯ

"I'll get it!"

Leigh threw open the apartment door. A boy in a Western Union tunic stood on the other side, hand raised for another knock. "Telegram for Mr Paladin."

"Naturally." She sighed. "Damy! Telegram!"

Dressed only in pants and undershirt, he stepped from the bathroom. Ever since they'd fished him out the ocean he seemed to spend a hell of a lot of time in the tub. When she asked him, all he did was shake his head and mutter something about oysters.

Damy took the telegram and tipped the boy. Ripping open the envelope he quickly scanned the contents, brows furrowing deeper with each second.

Leigh closed the door on the departing boy. "Who's it from?"

"The Navy. Thanking us for all I did for the *SG-1*."

"So why the sour puss?"

"After all I did... Hah!"

She held out a hand. "C'mon, gimme."

He stuffed the telegram into her palm and stalked back to the bathroom. Intrigued, Leigh lit a cigarette and settled herself comfortably into a chair.

```
US Navy would like to thank you for your efforts on its
                            behalf.
    All crew members recovered and returned to duty.
Submarine SG-1 trials considered complete. Soon to be
                        commissioned.
In your honor, all agreed boat to be named USS Oswin.
          Admiral Standley, Chief of Naval Operations
```

Leigh tried not to giggle. "You think they'll let me attend the ceremony?" she called. "You know – break a bottle of champagne over it?"

Out of the bathroom came his irate, muffled response: "After all I did!"

ECHOES OF DAYS PASSED

May 4th 1936: North Atlantic
Somewhere south of Reykjavik

Bendix grabbed at the rigging as the deck heaved without warning. He clung on a moment, watching the grey sea. There was very little swell. In fact they might have been in the doldrums, the water was so placid. A dismal mist hung in the air, reducing visibility to no more than a hundred yards. Bendix had no idea what had caused the small ageing fishing boat to pitch so badly and abruptly. There were no reefs out here – not unless they were ridiculously lost. The seabed should be at least two hundred feet below the keel.

The old boat calmed, sitting on the still water with all the grace of a sodden cardboard box. Bendix glanced over the side. It was like ink down there: nothing to see.

He made his way to the wheelhouse, sliding open the door and stepping inside. It wasn't much warmer, and instead of mist there was the fragrant murk of pipe smoke. Fisk was hunched over an array of electrical paraphernalia that had no place in a fishing boat's wheelhouse: two of the latest wireless receivers, a barograph, an innocent looking box which Bendix knew was fitted to hydrophones, and a set of cylinders and wires that included a continuous strip of graph paper along which three pens were dragging inky lines. One of the pens had just traced an enormous peak. Fisk was looking at it, the pipe clenched in his teeth twitching in time with the pens.

"That's not the target, is it?" said Bendix, peering over the other man's shoulder.

Fisk stared hard at the trace. A column of smoke signals rose from his pipe. "No," he murmured thoughtfully. "That isn't due for at least thirteen or fourteen minutes."

Bendix pointed at the single peak, now halfway to being wound around the end cylinder. "Then what was it?"

Fisk shrugged. "Nothing, most likely. I'd just switched on the equipment – making sure it was warmed up in time. Just a random spike."

Bendix didn't like random things. That spike coincided with the boat's sudden wallow. "Not a whale?"

"Did you happen to see a whale while you were out on deck?" Fisk's tone told Bendix exactly what he thought of that idea. Fisk held his hands wide apart. "Big thing. Exhales clouds of wet fishy breath. No, lieutenant, it's an artifact. Neither of the other detectors registered anything."

"Does ASDIC normally play up like that?"

Fisk shrugged again. "It's an improvement on the standard echo location system. More powerful, more sensitive. Problems are to be expected." He puffed out another cloud of smoke. "That's why we're here."

The lieutenant knew better than anyone why they were pretending to be fishermen out in the North Atlantic, miles from anywhere. Which reminded him. "Better check in with our opposite number."

He switched on one of the wireless sets and hit the transmit button. "Gemini Two calling Gemini One. Over." Bendix waited several seconds before trying again. "Gemini Two calling Gemini One. Do you read me? Over." There was nothing but a faint popping crackle. He would have checked the frequency but both radios had been pre-set and locked.

"What are they doing out there?" Bendix muttered. It was unlike Captain Travers to leave wireless telegraphy unmanned. "Come in Gemini One, this is Gemini Two. Are you receiving? Over." He glanced at his wristwatch: nine minutes or so before the target was in range. He needed Gemini One's confirmation that the sub was on its way – or a delay signal if something had come up. "Hello Gemini One, this is—"

The fishing boat lurched again. Bendix stumbled, almost falling over Fisk. He had time to note all three pens were thrashing across the moving paper, marking ever increasing spikes as the experimental ASDIC equipment responded to something.

The boat rolled. Bendix was thrown through the open wheelhouse door. He fetched up hard against the ship's rail, the breath driven out of him. He began to slide down the deck: the vessel's stern was going down. The sea – no longer calm – was foaming over the rail. They'd struck something and were sinking.

The bow rose. Bendix snatched for the side rail. He was no longer just sliding to stern – he was all but hanging. The trawler stood upright, sinking vertically into a sea that beat and thrashed against it. The water was seconds away from him. Bendix would have to try and swim free or be dragged down by the ship.

The wheelhouse was now above him. Bendix glanced up. Fisk was halfway out of the door, flapping like a beached fish. He looked as terrified as Bendix. The boat shook again. Bendix yelled in pain as his hands were almost torn free.

Above him, Fisk was struggling, trying to prise himself free of the wheelhouse. He slipped and tumbled. His flailing body crashed into Bendix, almost knocking him free. Then Fisk was gone.

Bendix looked at the pounding swirl that was drawing ever closer. He told himself there wasn't really something like a huge claw just below the surface, digging at the deck. That the trawler wasn't sinking – it was being dragged down. When the water was within a few feet of his dangling legs Bendix's pain-racked fingers lost their grip. He fell. Straight towards the maelstrom. Just before he hit water a cavern lined with vast curved daggers rose out of the surf, engulfing him.

CȜßᴐ

May 7ᵗʰ 1936: The Labrador Sea
Somewhere east of Newfoundland.

Commander Brad Munrow leaned negligently against the bridge rail as the submarine cruiser *USS Oswin* floated in an Atlantic that was presently showing its good side. He was scanning the clear sky with binoculars. The afternoon sun turned the ocean a deep blue. Tiny waves lapped the sub's four hundred foot long hull.

Munrow tweaked the binoculars' focus wheel. A dot grew sharper. "Plane, Captain. Far, two eight zero, elevation four, approaching."

Beside him, Captain Bannon pushed back his cap and raised his own field glasses. "I see it, Brad. Better get the welcoming committee on deck." There was an edge to his voice.

Munrow couldn't tell if it was excitement or apprehension. "One welcoming committee coming up." The commander unsealed a watertight hatch and removed the talker phone handpiece secured inside. "Control, this is the bridge. Break out the gangplank, Chief. Our visitor's here." He replaced the handset. "Any idea why the brass is paying us a visit?" The brief signal they'd received that morning hadn't been too big on details.

Bannon lowered his binoculars. "This boat's been something of a pet project for Admiral Corrigan. I guess he wants to be sure I'm taking care of it."

A hatch opened on the rear deck and two sailors hauled a collapsible gangway out, manhandling it carefully into position. Bannon and Munrow stowed their binoculars and made their way down via external steps aft of the bridge.

The plane circled to land. Sunlight flashed off its silver fuselage as it came down on the sea. It was a Douglas Dolphin, a twin-engined Navy amphibian, big enough for a half-dozen passengers. Or a single admiral.

The plane taxied towards the sub, engines blipping. As it came alongside the pilot rode the port wing float up onto the slope of the *Oswin's* main hull where it broke through the surface of the ocean, like the body of a huge whale.

The plane's hatch opened and the head of Admiral Rory Corrigan – unmistakable with the almost white spade beard covering its lower half – rose through it. He waved.

"Better get the gangway out now, boys," Munrow said to the crewmen. "Don't want to get the admiral's feet wet."

The admiral hauled himself up out of the plane and onto the gangway with the spriteliness of a man half his age. As he reached the *Oswin's* hull officers and men snapped to attention. One sailor piped Corrigan aboard. The admiral saluted briefly, turning to greet Captain Bannon. The two men shook hands, both grinning like old friends.

"Welcome aboard, Admiral," said the captain. He had to raise his voice as the airplane's engines revved. The gangway was disconnected, the plane turned, and the wash from its engines sprayed everyone on deck with a mist of seawater.

"He's in some kind of hurry!" Bannon yelled.

"Yeah, well I'm not officially here," Corrigan replied. "And he has to get my taxi back to Gander before it runs out of gas."

Bannon and Munrow shared a look. Yeah, thought the commander, the old man wants to play with the new toy.

Corrigan was taking in the *Oswin*. "Hard to imagine the Coast Guard has smaller cutters than this." His eyes fixed on the eight-inch twin-barrelled turret gun situated forward of the bridge. "And not so well armed."

"Few subs are, sir," said Bannon. "Shall we get below?"

"Of course. After you, Captain."

Bannon led Admiral Corrigan inside the boat. Corrigan whistled as he passed through the command centre.

"It's one thing to look at the blueprints, quite another to see it in the flesh. Pretty sure you could fit the old subs I served on in '18 inside of this tub and not even notice." He waved at the crewmen standing to attention. "At ease. This is no official visit so don't treat me any better than you would your captain." He winked at Bannon. "Well. Maybe a little better."

"Officers' quarters are below, sir," said Munrow. "This way."

As Bannon ordered the *Oswin* to get under way Munrow led the admiral down to the lower deck. The quarters were snug, with ten tiny cabins arranged around the wardroom.

"We have eight serving officers in total," said Munrow. "They've been ordered to keep it down. Your cabin is the most isolated so you shouldn't be too disturbed."

Corrigan looked inside the shoebox-sized room. He turned to Munrow with an easy smile. "Don't worry about me, son. This place is a palace compared to some of the sardine cans I've served on."

"If you say so, sir. Also, Captain Bannon wondered if the admiral would care for a tour of the boat..."

"You bet, Commander, but I've had a tiring day. Maybe tomorrow?"

"Very well, sir. Is there anything else?"

"Thank you, but you can quit worrying about this particular old man. And please tell Dave – Captain Bannon – the same, would you?"

"Whatever you say, Admiral." Munrow saluted. "I'll see you tomorrow."

Corrigan returned the salute. "Look forward to it, son."

CS80

The admiral had seen pretty much every inch of the sub. Since Corrigan had been involved with the conception and design of the *Oswin* from the get-go, Captain Bannon let him have a full inspection. They wound up in the spare aft section, where auxiliary bunks had been fitted for another forty people, on top of the one hundred and eight crew. Bannon sometimes wondered just who the designers imagined the sub would be taking on board. The *Oswin* wasn't some pleasure cruiser.

Admiral Corrigan leaned against an end bunk and took out a cigarette case. He offered a smoke to Bannon but the captain refused. Instead he stuck a half-smoked cigar between his teeth but didn't light it.

Corrigan blew out a cloud of smoke. "Well, Dave, up to now you haven't asked me why I'm here."

Bannon shrugged. "I figured you'd tell me if I needed to know. Wanting to be with your baby on her first voyage. Something like that."

Corrigan ran a hand down his beard. "Sure. And I'm glad to see she's performing so well."

"But...?"

The admiral smiled. "Am I that obvious?" He took a creased scrap of paper from a shirt pocket. "We intercepted this signal five days ago. It was encoded, of course, but using an old cipher we've known for years."

"Where from?" Bannon was thinking Nazi Germany.

"Iceland. The British Royal Navy are carrying out a low-level exercise up there."

Bannon took out his stogie and examined the chewed wet end. "How does that concern us?"

"Our information is, they're using fishing boats and an old wartime sub to test some new echo location gear. And being damned hush-hush about it."

"And...?" Bannon slipped the cigar back in his mouth.

"This boat has the most advanced echo-location equipment our boys can come up with." Corrigan's voice dropped to a whisper. "If the Brits have made breakthroughs, we'd like to know about it."

"You want we should just sail up there and ask them?"

Corrigan stroked his beard, half-smiling. "Three days ago they went quiet. Abrupt radio silence. The *Oswin* was already en route for the Arctic Circle and it seemed like an opportunity to pop by. See if they needed help."

Bannon did a quick calculation. "I reckon we're still over a day from Iceland. Their own boys will be out looking already."

Corrigan shook his head. "So far the Royal Navy have done nothing. Probably weighing their options, trying not to be noticed. If they send out a whole bunch of ships, the entire world will know."

"Sounds like half the world already knows."

"We got lucky. Our concern is that Germany might also get lucky."

Bannon glanced from the scrap in the admiral's hand to Corrigan's face. "What was their position when they went quiet?"

"I don't have an exact fix but I can narrow it down to twenty or thirty square miles."

"That's still a lot of water, Admiral."

Corrigan grinned and crushed out his cigarette. "And this big new boat's the best thing to cover it, Captain." He jammed the scrap back into his shirt. "The very best."

♋

Admiral Corrigan slipped out of the officers' quarters. He made no sound, sure that safe in their own cabins, neither captain nor commander heard a thing. Carefully, the admiral climbed the companionway to the upper deck, not slipping on his shoes until he was immediately outside the command centre. He stepped inside.

Even though he'd kept abreast of the construction of the *SC-1* – to use her original designation – from the moment her keel had been laid he couldn't get used to how roomy it was. Centralising features like periscope and steering alongside stations normally situated in the control room – such as diving and pressure – all in the upper deck resulted in the kind of breathing space Corrigan and his shipmates could only have dreamed of back in the Great War. The boat's commander had pretty much everything he wanted in sight and within reach of his voice. Even the radio room was close by, tucked in aft of the periscope.

For a moment, everyone on the night watch was oblivious to his presence. Then a guy in navy khaki – a CPO, Corrigan saw from his insignia – glanced up from a map laid across the chart table. Instantly he snapped to attention.

"Admiral on deck!"

As the crew came to their feet, Corrigan raised a hand. "Easy boys. As you were. I'm not here, remember?" He gave them all a wide friendly smile.

They settled back to their stations, murmuring among themselves. Corrigan strolled up to the chart table, trying not to look like he was studying the map, and spoke to the CPO. "Would it be possible for me to witness a dive? I'm curious as to how a boat this size handles underwater."

The chief, who looked to be around thirty even though his cropped hair already showed signs of grey, frowned, uncertain. "I should clear that with the captain, sir."

Corrigan's smile grew wider. "I doubt Captain Bannon would object. Just a dip below the waves. Humour an old man, Chief."

"Vallone, sir." He hesitated a moment before going to the talker phone. "Bridge, this is command centre. We're running a test dive in four minutes."

"Test dive in four, aye."

"Rig for dive."

As the admiral waited, all of the submarine's compartments reported back they were rigged for dive.

"Very well," acknowledged Vallone. "Clear the bridge."

"Bridge cleared." Seconds later a junior lieutenant dropped smartly down into the command centre, dogging the hatch above him, and took position at diving control.

"Very well. Dive, dive, dive."

Corrigan felt the unmistakable dip as the boat blew her buoyancy tanks. The sound of waves engulfing the hull echoed around him. It was a sound he sorely missed.

"Pressure in the boat," the lieutenant at diving control called. "Green board."

"Six-five feet," ordered Vallone. "Open bulkhead flappers and start ventilation."

One by one the compartments called back that the ventilation had started.

"Final trim six-five feet," reported diving control.

"Very impressive, Chief," said Corrigan. He moved to the port side, standing behind the hydrophone and echo location operators. Both men glanced around nervously, but Corrigan simply gave them a smile and a wave. "Carry on, gentlemen."

The hydrophones operator slipped headphones over his ears, adjusting controls. The EL operator – another junior lieutenant – did nothing.

"You not going to switch anything on, lieutenant?"

The operator looked back up at Corrigan again. "EL is activated only when likely to be needed, sir. We're in open water. Apart from a chance whale, there's nothing out here for the gear to respond to."

"Hydrophones enough, eh?"

"If the 'phones pick anything up the captain would order EL to be activated. The equipment's still experimental..."

"Yes. And one of the *Oswin*'s ongoing tasks is to test it, lieutenant. As a favour, just show me what it can do – but keep it simple, eh?"

The lieutenant shrugged, turned a control and two circular green screens began to glow. Tweaking another two knobs brought up two bright lines on each. As the equipment warmed a series of sine waves began to march across the upper line on both screens.

"Like oscilloscopes," commented the admiral.

The lieutenant nodded, adjusting one screen so the image was sharper. "Pretty much, sir. The waves show each sound pulse as it's generated. This is the forward projector, this the aft. Any echoes coming back at us will be registered on the lower trace. Amplitude can be used to measure the range, while these—" he tapped a series of dials "—indicate heading and depth. They're linked to the hydrophones."

"What's the maximum range?"

"That's one of the things the *Oswin* aims to determine, Admiral. Several thousand yards in theory."

"Better than the British ASDIC?"

"I wouldn't know, sir."

"Pretty powerful, though."

"We're advancing all the time, Admiral."

The upper trace on one of the screens blipped, a ragged curve sliding right to left. There was a second. And a third.

Corrigan leaned forward. "What's that?"

The lieutenant shook his head, tweaking a couple of knobs. "You got me, Admiral. It's big – far too big." He consulted the dials, shook his head again, and turned to the hydrophones operator. "What you make of it?"

The 'phones operator shrugged. "Could be a thermocline, but it appears to be moving. And fast."

Corrigan was intrigued. He hadn't imagined he'd actually get a chance to witness the EL gear in proper use. "What's the heading?"

The lieutenant glanced at a dial. "Straight for us, sir."

"If that's a whale, it's one for the record books," muttered the 'phones operator.

"Another sub?" The ragged echo traces on screen were growing in amplitude. Even Corrigan could figure what that meant. "It's almost on us! What's the range?"

"Seconds away, sir. It's going to—!"

A hollow moan belled though the hull. Corrigan felt the impact through his feet. The sub rolled to starboard by a degree or so. It sounded as though something huge and soft was pressed against the pressure hull, squeezing its way aft.

It fell silent. The boat righted.

"Is it gone?" asked Corrigan.

The lieutenant checked everything. "Yes, it's— No, it's coming about!"

"That's no sub!" muttered the 'phones operator.

A moment later the boat rang as though struck by a titanic hammer. It shuddered again, heeling over to port as whatever was out there rubbed against it.

"What the hell's going on!"

Corrigan turned at the voice. Captain Bannon was partway into the command centre, still half-dressed, holding on to a bulkhead doorframe as the sub bucked and pitched.

Chief Vallone, one hand on the periscope, came to attention. "Apologies, Captain, I—"

"Save it, Chief." Admiral Corrigan pushed himself across a deck that was still a degree or two off level. "I take full responsibility, Captain. I ordered a demonstration of the boat operating underwater."

Bannon said nothing, just pulled his cap on tight. He wouldn't want to cause a scene in front of the crew. He jammed his cold stogie between clenched teeth. "We'll talk about this later. Chief."

"Captain!"

"Make all preparations for surfacing. Check for leaks – on the double."

Commander Munrow appeared at the bulkhead door, shrugging into his shirt. "Somebody declare war—?" The surfacing alarm cut him off.

The captain put a hand on the ladder leading up to the bridge, pausing with one foot on a rung. "Open the main induction once the decks are visible. Brad – fetch a searchlight. And perhaps you'd like to join us, Admiral?"

Corrigan knew that wasn't a request. He followed up the ladder, with Commander Munrow close behind.

Outside it was still dark. Once all three were on the bridge Munrow plugged a large Klieg light into the sub's power supply, fitted it onto the guard rail, and flicked it on. A powerful beam swept the ocean.

The Atlantic was fitful, throwing black waves over the deck. Foam glowed in the searchlight. They heard nothing outside the sounds of the boat's diesel engines and the splash of waves.

"So what's the deal, Admiral?" asked Bannon, softly.

"I just wanted to see how she operated." Corrigan didn't sound convincing, even to himself.

"No thoughts of trying to sneak up on the Royal Navy's operations unseen, I suppose."

"Captain, let me assure you—"

"Stow it, Admiral. For now we have a boat to check over." His eyes followed the sweeping Klieg beam. "So what did we hit?"

Corrigan puffed out a breath that gleamed in the reflected searchlight. "Your boys seemed to think it hit *us*."

Bannon bit down on his cigar. "Whale?"

"Too big. Too manoeuvrable."

"Then what?"

"Captain." Commander Munrow was pointing. The searchlight caught something ten degrees to starboard. It gleamed in the light, slipping below the restless waves. Phosphorescence glowed in its wake.

"Sure looks like a whale to me," muttered Bannon.

Munrow kept the searchlight on the water, panning back and forth. After several seconds something broke the surface again, about thirty feet from the submarine's starboard beam. Corrigan had to agree with Captain Bannon: it looked like a big whale arching through the swell.

Except, in the Klieg's harsh light its sides looked pale, oily – even scaled.

Whatever it was, it sank out of sight as it headed past the bridge. A huge fluke rose above the waves, poised for a moment, sluicing water.

"That can't be right," Corrigan murmured. Unless his eyes were getting old and unreliable, the fluke looked more like a fish's tail. One that was something like twenty feet across. It smacked the water as it sank, creating a wash which momentarily flooded the deck.

"Tell me you both saw that." The admiral looked at captain and commander. Their expressions answered his question.

"That's one hell of an anchovy," breathed Munrow.

The sea erupted. Something breached. Something that reared over the bridge, staring down at them with cuttlefish eyes set in a skeletal face that was a perversion of human. A medusan nest of thick tendrils writhed from its skull. Its mouth gaped. Fangs the size of Roman pillars gleamed in the searchlight. It raised pale scaley arms, reaching toward the bridge with harpoon-sized talons set in steam-shovel paws.

For a frozen instant no one and nothing moved. Then something buried deep inside Corrigan's mind began to wail. The huge thing sank by degrees, never taking its strange eyes off the sub, until it had vanished below the black water. Corrigan began to breathe again.

Commander Munrow laughed: a timid, scared noise. "Always did want to see a mermaid."

☙❧

Back inside the command centre, Bannon stood at the chart table with Munrow and Corrigan. "Did we just see that – or are we all crazy?"

Corrigan shook his head. "Both hydrophones and echo-location picked it up."

"They picked *something* up," agreed Bannon.

"You spot anything else out there?" asked Munrow.

"God forbid there's another," Bannon sighed. "Chief ... are we okay to get under way?"

"Damage control reports nothing beyond bruises and a picture of some guy's girl that fell off a bunk," called Vallone.

"Then proceed on original course."

"And hydrophones, keep listening out for ... anything," added Munrow.

The EL operator tapped his rig. "Sir, I shut the dorsal projectors down when we surfaced, but we do have an experimental ventral array. It's not directional, but what it lacks in accuracy it more than makes up for in sheer volume. If you follow."

"Good idea, lieutenant," said Bannon. "You and 'phones keep a weather eye out."

Corrigan leaned forward. "Captain, I—"

"Later, Admiral. You can explain when we get back at Norfolk."

"Captain," called hydrophones. "Something out there. Large. Moving fast."

Dammit! Bannon mouthed. "Very well. EL: can you get a fix?"

"Far as I can tell, it's directly below us, sir. Approximately five hundred feet – and rising."

"Very well. Chief, rig for impact."

Before Vallone could give the order the whole sub shuddered, rolling to port as it was struck from below. Bannon hung onto the chart table with both hands. "Get us out of here, Chief! Full speed!"

The *Oswin* yawed. Something had the boat by the bow. Bannon sure as hell wasn't about to call that *something* a mermaid. He pushed himself off the table. "Up periscope! Darken command centre."

As he grabbed the rising periscope the lights dimmed. Looking forward over the turret gun, his eyes adjusting, he tried to make out something – anything – in the darkness. And there it was: a vast silhouette against a not quite black sky. Hulking over the sub's bow, holding onto it like it was some kid's toy in a bathtub.

He stepped back. "Down 'scope. Battle stations – gun action! Gun crew to fire control." He looked round at Munrow. "Man the bridge, Commander. Time we gave our main guns a test firing."

"Aye, Captain." Munrow began to climb.

Corrigan looked at Bannon, almost pleading. "We need to stop them—" he murmured. "It."

Bannon gazed at the admiral's drawn face. His skin was almost as white as his beard. There was a fever in his pale eyes that the captain didn't like the look of. "Okay, Admiral. You wanted to watch this tub in action, now's your chance."

They climbed up to the bridge as fast as they could. Munrow was already there, Klieg light back on. The beam played over the towering, scaled creature, still grasping the sub's bow in its huge paws. Bannon grabbed the talker phone.

"Fire control. Target is – directly ahead. Bearing zero zero. Range one double-zero."

"Zero zero, one double-zero. Aye."

"Commencing firing."

Both barrels of the eight-inch guns fired, the report deafening. Almost instantly the shells impacted, hitting the creature square in the teeth. It bellowed – a roar even louder than the guns – and fell back into the ocean. Waves foamed across the bow.

"Cease firing. Manoeuvring, steer course two zero."

"Did we get it?" Admiral Corrigan stared at the white-tops.

"We hit it," said Bannon. As for whether that was enough, he had his doubts.

"Starboard!" called Munrow. A huge plume of water erupted amidships. It was back and clearly not dead. A skeletal head gazed down on the bridge, its face a mess. Chunks of flesh were blown away, turning its mouth into a bloody snarl, teeth on one side exposed in a rictus grin. The thick tendrils on its head writhed, some oozing a dark fluid. Its strange cuttlefish eyes glared with pain – or fury.

"Can't bring the deck gun to bear," muttered Bannon. It was too far aft.

Munrow stepped back from the searchlight. "The AA gun!"

"Brad!"

The commander was already half sliding down a companionway aft of the bridge. He reached the deck mounted anti-aircraft gun, swivelling to aim up at the colossal shape looming over the sub. Bannon played the searchlight over the thing, giving Munrow something to aim at. The creature glistened, shades of blue and green, refracted light sparkling off its scales.

Munrow opened fire. The thing twitched and bellowed. Bannon could see the impact lines stitching across the scaled torso, but they were about as effective as pitching rocks at an elephant. It just got madder and reached forwards, flinching with every hit. An arm swept down, batting at the AA gun's barrel. Munrow was swatted aside, slipping on the wet deck. He vanished into the darkness.

"Brad!" Bannon started for the rear companionway.

Corrigan grabbed him by the arm. "I'll see to him! Command this boat, Dave!"

Before the captain could argue the admiral was making his way down to the deck, muttering incoherently as he descended.

The mer-thing had lost interest in the AA gun now it had fallen silent, its ruined face turned left and right as if it was looking for something. It sank, almost up to its oddly jointed arms, slapping at the sub's hull. Bannon winced at each blow. Too many of them and the *Oswin* would crack like a rotten log.

He called down the talker. "Manoeuvring, full astern."

The sub began to reverse, slipping past the looming thing. The creature seemed baffled at first, its shattered jaw hanging loose in a vacant expression. Then it surged forward with a deep rumble Bannon felt in his guts, crushing several feet of deck guardrail with a petulant swat.

On the rear deck, Corrigan was dragging Munrow's inert body back into the light. At least he hadn't gone overboard. The admiral shuffled clumsily, his head constantly swinging about to check on the half-submerged creature. It remained indifferent to both men, more interested in punching out the *Oswin*.

"Medical detail to the aft deck!" Bannon called down the talker. "On the double!"

Munrow was hidden from Bannon's sight now. At the foot of the companionway the captain hoped, and alive. Corrigan reappeared, shuffling towards the AA gun. Bannon leaned from the bridge. "Admiral, get back up here!"

Corrigan shook his head. He was still talking to himself, his words difficult to make out above the waves, the creature's rumbling, the sub's engines. "...All along ... fooled us ... me ... this was ... ASDIC..." He was laughing. "ASDIC! Last laugh, though ... take ... we'll get ... I'll get..."

Bannon watched as Corrigan took up position with the AA gun, handling it with the ease of a younger, fitter man. He fired, hitting the thing's injured head and left shoulder. It howled, leaving Bannon's ears ringing. The admiral fired again, keeping up a constant barrage. The creature was hurting. Its howls now ones of pain. Agony. It swiped at the sub, slapped the sea instead, drenching Corrigan. It hit out again, this time heeling over – capsizing. But it righted itself, shaking its head, its tendrils hanging limp.

Corrigan never let up, hammering the thing with every shot. Stinging it, wearing it down. Until his ammo ran out.

The thing had been falling back, increasingly reluctant to stay in range of the reversing sub. Now it surged forward again, porpoising, its scaley fishlike lower parts slapping the water.

Several crewmen were on the rear deck now, armed with automatics and machine guns. As the thing rose out of the water they fired in unison but the creature didn't even notice. Its attention was focussed on Corrigan, still manning the empty AA gun. It slammed a huge, webbed paw down. The admiral paused in his constant incoherent speech long enough to laugh again. Then the paw raked the deck, crushing, tearing. When the creature fell back into the water, the deck was empty of both AA gun and Corrigan.

"Rory!"

Bannon had to restrain himself from racing down to the deck. He couldn't help the admiral – not now – and he had a submarine to look after.

Machine gun and small arms fire were almost continuous. The creature was holding position, probably hurting badly. It sank down into the waves until only its ruined head showed, keening a mournful whale-like song that reverberated through the water. Gradually, the *Oswin* increased the gap between them, all the while Bannon keeping the searchlight trained on it, waiting for the moment when it came at them again.

He had a sudden crazy idea and picked up the talker phone. "Torpedo tracking party, man your stations. Forward room, order of tubes is one, two, three, four."

"Forward room, aye."

"Forward room make ready forward tubes. Set depth one-zero feet."

The creature still wasn't moving. From what Bannon could make out it was treading water, watching the departing sub, contemplating its next move. Or was he giving a dumb monster too much credit?

"Forward room ready to fire."

"Very well." The thing was around two hundred feet away now, around half the length of the sub, although it still stood out clearly in the searchlight beam. "EL: do you still have it on track?"

"Aye, Captain – but I wouldn't bet my paycheck on the positioning."

"We can see it, lieutenant. Do you have the amplitude up full?"

"It won't increase the accuracy—"

"Give it everything you got."

"Everything we've got, aye."

"Stop engines!"

The *Oswin* slowed. Above the slap of waves on the hull Bannon could hear the medical detail taking Munrow below, armed crewmen making their way forward around the sub's superstructure. The thing ahead moaned, its cries flat and muffled by the choppy sea.

"Come on you son-of-a-bitch," Bannon muttered.

Its head quirked. If it had ears, the captain imagined it alternating them, trying to zero in on a certain sound. It howled, surging forward like a swimmer pushing off a poolside.

"Got your attention! Forward room. Fire one! Fire two!" Bannon imagined he saw the wakes as the fish burst from their tubes.

The creature plunged below the sea. In the searchlight the captain could just make out the bow-wave as it surged towards the sub.

The sea drummed. A second later it geysered up in an explosion of foam. The creature's head and shoulders surfaced a moment afterwards. It was screaming. Water and blood poured off it.

"Fire three. Fire four!"

Both struck the thing square, ripping into it. Tearing it apart. What remained collapsed into the churning waves. There was no more eerie howls.

"That's for Rory Corrigan, you bastard," murmured Bannon.

∞

Munrow stood, buttoning his shirt. Bannon was standing in the door of the cramped sickbay, arms folded, his expression leagues away.

"Doc says I'm fine, Captain." The commander picked up his cap. "Few bruises. Nothing broken. Better shape than the sub, anyhow. We returning to Norfolk for repairs?"

Bannon nodded.

"Listen, I—" Munrow shuffled his cap in both hands. "I'm sorry about the admiral, sir. I guess you and he were old friends—"

"Thanks, Brad." The captain shook his head, back in the present. "Reckon he died saving the sub – or so the log will record."

They left the sickbay together, walking back towards the command centre. "Speaking of which, what *was* that?" wondered Munrow.

Bannon shrugged. "Sailors have been seeing mermaids for centuries – human sized ones. Maybe the longer they live, the bigger they get."

"Swell thought. So why did it attack us?"

"Maybe it was the echo location gear. It seemed to pretty much ignore us when it wasn't switched on. I had EL turn the amplitude way up and even though it must have been hurting it came back at us." He dug around in a shirt pocket and produced his cold stogie, popping it between his teeth. "The admiral told me about a Royal Navy mission off the Iceland coast that went silent a few days ago. They were testing some new ASDIC equipment..." His voice tailed off.

"You think they ran into tall dark and ugly?"

"Something like that. I wouldn't like to think there was another one out there."

"Amen to that," said Munrow with conviction.

CﳀꗄꙆ

A hundred miles south of Reykjavik, settled on the continental shelf, a dozen opaque packets, each the size of a suitcase, waited in the cold nutritious waters. Nestled inside rocky clefts and held in place by thin tendrils growing from their corners, each held a small dark shape. Occasionally, each would wriggle and thrash, testing the walls of their eggs with sharp claws.

DRAWING DOWN
LEVIATHAN

Captain Bannon glanced across the control room at his Number One. "Mister Munrow?"

Commander Munrow raised his dark eyes from a stopwatch. "Three minutes."

"Very well. Come to periscope depth."

The submarine cruiser *USS Oswin* rose gently, the movement barely registering under the captain's feet.

"Periscope depth!"

"Very well. Up 'scope." Bannon grabbed the periscope handles and made a full sweep of the ocean before fixing on the silhouette of a distant heavy cruiser. Almost broadside on to the submarine, the ship seemed unaware of the sub's presence. All four spotter planes were absent from the deck – no doubt looking for the *Oswin*. In the wrong place, Bannon hoped.

He grabbed the talker phone. "Battle stations torpedo. Forward room, order of tubes is one, two, three."

"Forward room one, two, three, aye."

"Make ready forward tubes. Set depth zero eight feet."

"Zero eight feet, aye."

"Forward room, fire one, two and three.

"Torpedoes away!"

Bannon heard the double click of Brad Munrow's stopwatch.

"Impact in eleven seconds..."

Bannon found himself counting down, hoping he wasn't racing the clock.

"Impact!"

Through the periscope the heavy cruiser had made no evasive manoeuvre. If the *Oswin* had fired three torpedoes for real, the ship out there would be in serious trouble.

"Forward room, reload tubes one, two—"

"That won't be necessary, Captain."

Bannon stepped back from the 'scope, looking aside at the one who had spoken: a scrawny lieutenant in navy khaki, carefully making notes on a clipboard. "If you're sure, Mr Downs?"

The other man smiled. Even that was thin. "I think we may assume the *Chester* is either sinking or disabled, Captain Bannon – just like the other two Northampton cruisers this boat successfully attacked during the exercise. Bravo."

Bannon shrugged. "Forward room, belay that order. Secure from battle stations. Down 'scope, and make all preparations for surfacing." Fishing in his shirt pocket for the cold, half-smoked cigar he habitually kept in there, he added, "And RT, signal the commander of the *USS Chester* once we're up." He grinned. "Send my compliments, and say I hope there are no hard feelings."

∝≫

Bannon and Munrow stood on the *Oswin's* forward deck, leaning on the bow rail. Above and behind them loomed both barrels of the submarine's eight-inch gun turret. In the distance the *USS Chester* was steaming slowly sou-southwest, Lieutenant Downs safely back on board. Two of its spotter planes were also back in position, the remainder to be picked up en route to the Panama Canal.

"Guess the brass will be happy now." Bannon chewed on his stogie.

"Not sure 'happy' is the word I'd use, sir," said Munrow. "We've demonstrated that a sub capable of diving deep enough to avoid aerial reconnaissance can disable three of our most recent heavy cruisers in one run. If this had been for real, eastern access to the Panama Canal would be pretty compromised."

Bannon laughed. "That's kind of the point of exercises, mister."

There was an amplified hail from the bridge. Munrow turned round. "What was that?" he yelled.

"Plane, commander!" the officer on watch called through a megaphone. "Far, one one zero, elevation four, approaching."

Munrow raised his eyes, shielding them to see better. There was a smudge against the clear Caribbean sky, growing darker and clearer.

"We got company." He pointed up at the approaching dot.

"One of the *Chester's* remaining seaplanes?" wondered Bannon. "Didn't realise her captain was such a sore loser." He was already heading aft. Munrow fell in behind him. They climbed up to the bridge where the lieutenant on watch handed Bannon his binoculars. The captain gazed up at the shape before handing the glasses to Munrow.

"What you make of it, Brad?"

The commander focused. It was still difficult to make out, little more than a grey blur against the blue sky. "Nothing I recognise," Munrow admitted.

"Get below," Bannon ordered the watch. "Sound general quarters and rig for dive."

"Aye, sir." The lieutenant descended out of sight.

"Don't want the *Chester* – or any of the other ships – catching us with our pants down," murmured Bannon. "Trying to sneak in a last-minute air assault while we're standing around slapping each other on the back."

"Hardly in the spirit of the exercise," Munrow commented.

"Maybe. But the spotter crew can brag they sunk the boat which torpedoed their own ship." He winked at the commander. "Hell, it's what I'd do."

The talker phone buzzed. *"Boat's ready to dive, Captain."*

"Very well."

The distant airplane was growing clearer, almost sharp enough to see without binoculars. "Looks big enough to be a commercial plane," Munrow said, half to himself.

Bannon frowned "We're way off any local flight routes."

The approaching silhouette grew larger. It was big, Munrow realised, real big. "If it wasn't moving so fast and had wings, I'd say it was a zeppelin," he muttered.

It seemed to be some kind of huge flying boat, nearly all trailing vee wing, with twin hulls attached to the underside. There seemed to be a smaller vee above the main one, and although he couldn't be sure, Munrow thought he could make out something like a dozen engines mounted along its leading edge. He could certainly hear the high drone of multiple props.

"It's like something cooked up by Le Corbusier. Or Bel Geddes,"

Bannon glanced at him. "If you say so, mister. But I'd bet a month's pay it's not one of ours. Something European? Germany, maybe?"

"If it was the Nazis, they'd have told the world already."

The huge airplane dropped lower. Now Munrow could see the main wing's leading edge was dotted with windows or portholes; the nose section alone had four rows. The twin hulls both had five rows of small portholes on either side, like two miniature passenger ships. A broad, flat cockpit was perched on top of the nose like some kind of Modernist glasshouse. The plane dropped to within a hundred feet of sea level, passing over the *Oswin*, starboard wing dipped as the pilot took a good, hard look. The machine seemed too big and slow to be able to stay up, its shadow enveloping the sub for a moment. The roar of multiple engines was almost overpowering. As it banked away, Munrow saw the dorsal wing had even more engines fixed to its trailing edge.

"You sure that's not one of Howard Hughes's daydreams?" said Bannon. "It's one big ugly flying boat."

"More like a flying ocean liner," Munrow admitted. "A real leviathan."

The plane banked to the left, flying sedately eastwards. Munrow allowed himself to relax. Then it changed course. The flying boat banked again, coming broadside on to the sub, twin hulls only a couple of dozen feet above the waves. Commander Munrow didn't like it. Not one bit.

He grabbed the talker phone. "Belay dive! General quarters! AA crew hit the deck, at the double!"

Moments later, aft of the bridge, two crewmen appeared on deck, manning the anti-aircraft gun. They swung it around, bringing it to bear on the approaching plane.

The sea around the submarine's hull erupted into a flurry of small geysers. Munrow heard the *spang!* of ricocheting bullets. He ducked, just having time to notice a couple of portholes in the wings were spitting flame.

The AA team didn't wait for further orders. They opened up on the closing airplane. Munrow raised his head above the bridge sides, watching the occasional tracer shell arc towards the colossal flying boat.

The plane roared overhead, the undersides of its hulls looking close enough to touch. The AA crew swung their gun around, holding fire just long enough to not blow captain and commander off the bridge. Tracer snaked after the departing plane. More machine gun fire stuttered from the wings' trailing edges.

There was a burst of thick black smoke from the banks of aero engines, twisting in the backwash. The huge plane banked ponderously and there was another belch of smoke, followed by a brief streamer of flame. The flying boat continued turning, under fire all the time – although Munrow guessed it was beyond the range of the AA gun, and moving too fast. Wherever the gunnery crew had hit, they'd got lucky.

The plane levelled off, trailing two lines of smoke, and kept on going. The AA gun maintained a token barrage for a few more seconds until it was clear the flying boat was in retreat, wounded. After a minute it was no longer visible except for two fading smoke trails.

Munrow peered over the bridge, running a finger over punctured steel. He picked up the talker phone. "Control, secure from general quarters. All compartments report damage."

Hanging up the phone he turned to the captain. "Whoever they were, I guess we gave them a bloody nose." He poked the bullet hole again. "Though we took a few licks ourselves."

Bannon was staring hard after the disappeared flying boat. "Guess they won't be back in a hurry."

"What now?" said Munrow, although he was pretty sure of the answer.

"Obvious, Brad. I figure they're heading back to wherever they came from – while they still can. If the *Oswin's* up to it, we go find your leviathan's base."

CRBO

Bannon was in the control room, bent over the chart table, when CPO Vallone reported to him. "What's the word, chief?"

The grey-haired man gave a thin smile. "Damage control reports nothing below the waterline, Captain."

"That's something. Topside?"

"Bullet holes in the superstructure. Some scarring across the decks and upper hull. And we lost the radio mast."

"How long for repairs."

"Mast will take a couple of days – and that'll be a jury-rig. The rest will have to wait until we get back to Norfolk."

"And if we submerge?"

"No guarantees, sir. Pressure hull might spring a leak, or it might not."

"Swell." Bannon dropped the pencil he'd been toying with and glanced across the table at Munrow. "So we can't dive or report back home. Thanks, Chief. That'll be all."

Vallone saluted and left. Bannon went back to staring at the chart stretched across the table. "That plane was heading east when it first buzzed us, before coming back for the strafing run. After we damaged the engines, it headed pretty much due east again." He picked up the pencil and drew a big thick arrow on the chart. "What would you estimate the range on a thing like that might be, Brad?"

Munrow shrugged. "Anywhere between a thousand and fifteen hundred miles."

"My thoughts exactly." Bannon drew a semi-circle, centred on the sub's present position. It cut across a lot of empty ocean. "Fifteen hundred miles. Even with full tanks there's nothing out there within range."

"Uncharted islands?" suggested Munrow.

"Maybe – though the odds are against it. The plane could maybe make Bermuda – except I'm guessing it doesn't want to be seen..."

"You're thinking a carrier?"

"What kind of carrier could take something that big? Maybe a support vessel. A refuelling tanker. If they stayed off the shipping lanes and kept away from commercial flightpaths, like us, they could stay hidden a while. They likely weren't expecting to run across anything like the *Oswin*." He ran his fingertip along the pencilled arc, tapping where it and the thick arrow intersected. "I guess somewhere around here."

"We're going flying ocean liner hunting." Munrow was grinning.

Bannon smiled back. "Lookouts to the bridge, Brad. Manoeuvring, come about to zero eight nine. Best speed. And try not to get water in those bullet holes."

೦೩೮೦

Brad Munrow was sitting in the officer's wardroom when a call came over the talker circuit.

"Commander Munrow, report to the bridge."

He acknowledged the call, gulped his coffee, and climbed through the *Oswin's* two decks and up to the bridge. Captain Bannon was staring across the water. He handed Munrow his binoculars.

"Take a look, Brad."

Munrow focused. Just on the horizon was an indistinct shape. A grey shimmer. Too big to be the flying boat. "Your refuelling tanker?"

"If it is, it's bigger than any I've ever seen."

"A carrier after all?"

"Maybe." The captain took the glasses off Munrow and stared down them again. "The unknowns are stacking up, Brad. I don't like it."

"We going in closer?"

"What do you think? The *Oswin* has a low profile, and if we keep her bow forward she'll be hard to spot. Long as we keep our distance."

Munrow picked up the talker phone. "Manoeuvring, slow to one third."

"One third, aye."

"And once we're keeping our distance?" asked Munrow, hanging up the phone.

"It'll be dark in an hour or so," said the captain. "Guess someone ought to go take a closer look."

☙❦

Whatever it was, Munrow wouldn't call it a carrier. As the *Oswin* crept closer the light gradually faded, while the distant smudge grew more solid. And bigger. Even standing a little under a mile off, the vessel loomed against the twilight sky, black and angular.

It was as though someone had taken a ferry boat, stretched it to enormous size, and dumped half of Manhattan on top. There was no obvious bow or stern, and the only side the commander could make out was a towering blank wall, with no portholes or openings. Its silhouette looked more like a city skyline than that of a ship. There were even two conical towers, fore and aft – whichever was which – that could have been lighthouses. Neither were lit. If the vessel wanted to evade detection, that made sense. The *Oswin's* own running lights were dowsed after all.

Standing beside him on the bridge, binoculars to his eyes, Captain Bannon whistled. "How has no one spotted *that* before? It's – what? – a thousand feet long at the waterline."

The commander's own estimate was closer to fifteen hundred. "It must stand at least two hundred feet above the plimsol line. I doubt it could outmanoeuvre a paddle boat."

"Maybe it doesn't need to. A barge that size could carry some pretty impressive armament." The captain frowned. "Can you see a flag of any kind?"

Munrow raised glasses of his own and scanned the vessel end to end. "Nothing. But I can make out something kind of familiar over there." He pointed starboard, where a thick wing and the hint of a ship-sized hull were just visible behind the huge vessel's bulk. A minnow moored to a whale. The commander lowered his binoculars and lit a cigarette. "Like the man said, someone ought to go take a look."

Bannon took out his cigar and stared at the well-chewed end. "Who will you take?" he said after a pause.

"Chief Vallone – he has the boat's highest small arms rating. Seamen Slade and Caetano – both swim like fish and are too dumb to know when to quit."

The captain smiled. "Haven't thought about it much, have you?"

"Never had the time."

By the time one of the sub's two motorboats was unshipped from a watertight compartment under the deck aft of the AA gun it was almost full dark. The distant hulking vessel was no longer visible in the thin moonlight; its engines were silent. Chief Vallone and the two seamen reported – Slade, blond and looking too young to be in the Navy, and Caetano, dark and craggy – already armed with automatic pistols. Like Munrow, all three were dressed in dark turtlenecks and pants. The chief handed a holstered gun to Munrow.

Captain Bannon stood by the AA gun, watching carefully. "This has to be a quick out and back operation," he said. "We have no information who's crewing that ship, or who's behind it. But we do know they have a big, not so friendly airplane at their disposal. I think we can assume the crew's of a like mind."

"Understood, sir," said Vallone. "And what if the reception hots up?"

"Commander Munrow will use his discretion." Bannon popped the cold stogie back between his teeth.

They slipped the motorboat over the side, clambered on board and pushed off. As the motorboat's engines would be heard for miles, all four unshipped oars and began to row carefully. Munrow hoped the huge ship wouldn't suddenly come to life and decide to steam off before they could reach it.

After what felt like forever, a vast, shrouded bulk loomed out of the night. The ship's towering hull had been painted a smoky grey, so reflected little of the scant moonlight. They pulled alongside, nudging their small boat against the dark hull, searching for a way to climb on board. There was nothing until they reached the vessel's square bows, or stern – it could have been either. There was a wide, flat deck some fifteen to twenty feet above the water, opened ended, its trailing edge angled slightly upward. A companion ladder, set into the hull, led upward. Munrow climbed out of the motorboat before any of the others could volunteer. This was his show and he was going to lead from the front.

Reaching the deck he crouched a moment, listening hard. When he was happy he was alone he leaned over the edge, indicating to the three men in the boat below to come ahead. Seaman Slade grabbed for the ladder first, followed by Vallone and Caetano. Silently, they climbed up to join him.

They were standing in a vast space that resembled an aircraft hangar. Bulkhead lights, slightly dimmer than the thin exterior moonlight, gave off a dim glow. Barely enough for the commander to make out the roof overhead – some fifty feet up. Any light spillage would be barely noticeable, even in the moonlight. The distant side bulkhead was lost in shadow, just pinpricked by tiny bulkhead lights of its own.

Munrow listened some more. Aside from everyone's breathing he heard nothing. He pulled out a flashlight and flicked it on briefly. Hard to tell by torchlight, but he figured it had to be an enclosed flight deck – and it was huge. A space at least three times wider than its height that could probably hold a whole squadron of Grumman fighters and still have room for a mess hall.

"What do you make of it, commander?" whispered Vallone.

Munrow shook his head. The vessel seemed deserted. No airplanes and no crew. Just a huge, resonant silence.

They moved deeper inside, as softly as possible. Even breathing too loudly awoke faint echoes. The inner bulkhead was dotted with occasional watertight doors. They tried them all as they passed through the hanger. Each one was locked. By Munrow's estimation they had reached the huge deck's halfway point when he found another ladder, set into the bulkhead. Munrow flicked on his flashlight. The ladder went all the way past the roof. Must be a companionway to the next deck, or whatever was above.

"Anyone scared of heights?" he asked, putting away his flashlight and grabbing the rungs.

Normally Munrow could have shimmied up fifty feet in a few seconds. Now he took his time, careful not to make a sound, aware of the echoes. Below him, the rest were just as cautious.

There was a watertight hatch set in the deckhead above him. Slowly, Munrow spun the locking wheel one-handed, grateful whoever did the maintenance round here had been liberal with the grease. He raised the hatch an inch, peering through the gap. It looked like another hangar deck, pretty much identical to the one below – except the lighting was a tad brighter. He risked pushing the hatch open some more, squeezing his head and shoulders through. It was quiet. No one about. Just lines of crates and drums lashed to the deck, no more than a yard away.

And to his right, filling almost half of the deck, a huge flying boat, its fuselage resting in a massive cradle, tail section brushing against a plain bulkhead which sealed off the end of the flight deck. The tips of its single, overhead wing almost touched the bulkheads on either side. Six push-pull engine nacelles were mounted on the wing, and the commander couldn't miss the swastika painted on the tail.

Munrow clambered out and belly-crawled to the line of drums – gas cans, by the smell – hoping there was no one on board the flying boat who could spot him. Vallone, Slade and Caetano pulled themselves through after him. Munrow signalled them to keep down. All four peered at the huge airplane through gaps between the drums.

"That ain't our bird," hissed Caetano.

"It's a Dornier Do-X," Chief Vallone whispered. "How in hell did that get up here?"

Munrow looked up and around. Just above the Dornier, half-hidden in the poor light, was a heavy crane, running on rails the size of girders.

"They hauled it aboard. Somehow."

A metallic clang echoed across the hangar deck. The commander ducked automatically. He heard voices coming from across the hangar, speaking in English and growing louder, closer. Seconds later the voices' owners stepped into view below the Dornier's nose. One was dressed as an officer in Germany's *Luftwaffe,* another the *Kriegsmarine.* Several more, in simple coveralls, hurried aboard the flying boat. The crew, Munrow figured. The rest wore fancy brown get-ups the commander didn't recognise, although judging by the amount of gold braid adorning one of the men's caps, Munrow figured he had to be some kind of officer. The huge vessel's commander? The rest seemed to be just armed guards, carrying machine guns Munrow couldn't identify.

The one with all the braid was talking, fast and excited.

"—overall, I am sure you were satisfied with the demonstration." His voice was heavily accented, but his English clear.

The one in the *Luftwaffe* uniform pulled a sour expression. "It was impressive, *Herr* Araujo. Your aircraft has potential. However—"

The one he'd called Araujo held up his hands. "We have discussed this already, *Herr Oberst.* The pilot has been dealt with."

"Such action would not be necessary if your men were already sufficiently disciplined—" The *oberst's* voice was drowned by the roar of twelve engines erupting into life. "You will be hearing from Berlin shortly!" he yelled above the noise. He bowed curtly and quickly boarded the Dornier, the one in the *Kriegsmarine* uniform following closely.

"How they gonna get that bird in the air?" muttered Slade.

Munrow realised both ends of the deck ended in identical bulkheads. Now the one far away to his left and facing the Dornier was opening, swinging or folding out of the way. As it did so the lighting dimmed to a sullen glow. Within a minute the far end of the deck was just a black void.

The officer with all the scrambled eggs moved his men back. White puffs of vapour began to curl up from under the cradle in which the flying boat sat. Some kind of launching mechanism? Munrow wondered. Steam powered? The plane's twelve engines ran up to full power, the noise deafening in the enclosed space.

A moment later the cradle began to move forward, the Dornier riding it, picking up speed. Excess steam vented in plumes that shrieked even louder than the engines. Before it plunged over the edge of the deck the cradle came to an abrupt halt. The flying boat didn't stop. It slingshot through the deck's open end, engines howling. For a moment it dipped, dropping out of Munrow's vision. Then it reappeared, softly backlit by the deck's low lighting, climbing into the night.

⚭

"Captain! Forward lookout. To the bridge!"

Bannon acknowledged and rapidly ascended from the control room. Up on the bridge, the forward watch pointed ahead. A diffuse shaft of light shone into the night, off the sub's port bow. Like the beam of a distant failing flashlight. Bannon heard aeroengines. He grabbed a pair of binoculars.

He was in time to see an airplane spat out along the scattered light beam, appearing from nowhere. It rose, a grey smudge against the darkening sky, then faded into the darkness. Towards north, as far as Bannon could tell. The sound of engines dimmed. The shaft of faint light narrowed, like it was being gradually blanked off, finally winking out altogether.

Bannon lowered his glasses. "As if this job needed to get any crazier."

CらRO

The silence that fell over the hangar deck was almost absolute. It was broken by the staccato sounds of the officer and his men returning to the far bulkhead, boots loud on the deck surface. The lights faded further, to the same dim level as on the lower deck. Once the echoes of a door slamming had tailed off Munrow judged it safe to move. All four slipped out from behind the drums.

"What now, sir?" wondered Vallone.

Munrow glanced up towards the distant roof. "At a guess I'd say there's at least one more deck. Anyone curious about what's up there?"

Slade and Chief Vallone grinned an answer. Caetano just shrugged.

Carefully, feeling exposed on the wide deck despite the thin illumination, Munrow led them to the doorway through which the brown uniformed men had gone. They paused, all drawing their automatics, before the commander slowly cracked open the door. He waited a moment – no one yelled an alarm. He opened it further and slipped through, checking left and right. He was in a narrow grey passageway, lined with pipes, trunking, and bulkhead lights. From what he could see in their glow Munrow imagined they could be on board just about any navy ship.

"Which way?" muttered Slade.

Munrow checked up and down the passageway. They were pretty close to one end of the deck, so taking a left offered more possibilities. "Guess this way's as good as another." He pointed with his automatic.

They trod carefully, shoes tapping faintly on the metal deck. At least there were no echoes along here. They heard no one, saw no one.

After a half minute or so they reached a companionway. Signalling everyone to stay back, the commander edged forward, glancing up the stairwell. There was no one. The steps rose up, every ten feet or so switching back and forth through a series of small landings. About five in all, far as he could tell, before it reached the next deck. Nodding briefly to Vallone, Munrow started up the first flight.

There was a small door leading off the first landing, not locked. Behind was a storage space, empty. The door was numbered, with a single word underneath.

"Anyone read Spanish?" murmured Munrow, taking a guess at the language.

"A little," said Caetano. "Except that ain't Spanish. Not even Portuguese."

They climbed another two flights. The next door was numbered seventy-two, with the word *Armilêambro* stencilled on it. It was locked.

They crept up another two flights before reaching an open doorway leading into a passageway identical to the one they had left below.

Opposite was a closed bulkhead door. Munrow eased it open. Beyond was another flight deck. Signalling the rest to follow, he stepped over the raised lip and out onto the deck.

Just like the one below this had closed ends, with crates, drums and barrels lashed all along its length. Unlike the others it was open to the sky, letting in faint moonlight. Heavy arched beams spanned overhead, casting pale shadows across a half-dozen seaplanes lined up along the deck. All were twin-engined sesquiplanes. Amphibians, judging from the landing gear mounted below the boat-shaped underwing cabins. Machine gun barrels jutted from every upswept nose. More were mounted in the tail end of each cabin.

"Someone means business," said Vallone.

"Sleek sons of bitches, too," Slade commented.

He was right. The planes reminded Munrow of Sikorsky S-38s, but more stylish. All the angles had been smoothed to elegant curves, the struts to graceful arches. Even the twin-boom tails were swept back into soaring arcs. Like they'd been designed by an artist rather than an engineer.

If sharks could fly, the commander thought, they'd look like this. But where were the crews? In fact, where were all the men he'd expect to run a ship this size? So far they'd seen a only handful, and heard nothing.

"Think it's time we got off this bucket and reported back—"

The deck under Munrow's feet began to vibrate. He exchanged a look with Vallone. The chief was thinking exactly the same: the ship's engines had started up. If the huge vessel got underway the *Oswin* would certainly lose them in the dark.

The commander turned, meaning to make his way back to the bulkhead door they'd come through. It was blocked by the one in an officer's uniform and a couple of armed goons. The man was smiling easily, a slim automatic pointing generally at the sub's crew.

"Please lower your weapons. If you are thinking of running back to your little motorboat, let me assure you there is no need. It was discovered and cut adrift ten minutes ago." His smile widened. "I am

Generalkapitano Araujo of the *Flotego de Urboj*. Welcome to our flagship *La Estro*. I hope you will enjoy your stay."

⋘⋙

Captain Bannon heard the low throb of engines coming across the water. It could only mean one thing.

"Dammit! That ship's about to sail!" He grabbed the talker phone. "Hydrophones, can you get a fix on the departing ship's engines?"

There was far too long a pause. *"Bridge, this is hydrophones. We've got them—"*

"Echo location, can you track it?"

"Echo location, aye. I have the ship on the ventral projector. The track's pretty rough and ready, Captain. Be like playing Marco Polo underwater—"

"Just until dawn breaks and we get a decent visual."

"Aye, Captain."

"Manoeuvring, from now on until I countermand, take your heading from the EL station. Engine room, ahead one third. Once we're underway, hydrophones and EL have the con."

"Manoeuvring, aye."

"Engine room, aye."

Bannon hung up the phone and stared into the darkness.

⋘⋙

Commander Munrow looked around the cramped cabin. Every inch of it, from floor to wall and ceiling bulkheads, was painted in that pale battleship grey beloved of navies everywhere. A small round light in the ceiling gave off more harsh brilliance than anything that size had a right to. There was no chair, no table, not so much as a porthole. The only things to break the monotony were two narrow pipes running alongside the frame of the secured watertight door, outlined by stark shadows cast by the ceiling light.

He tried the door's locking wheel, but it was held fast from the other side. He leaned against the wall facing the door once pacing the deck had lost its novelty, wondering where his men were – how they were – and if the *Oswin* was managing to follow in the dark.

Occasionally he heard raised voices beyond his cell, all jabbering in some language he didn't recognise. Gaetano was right: it wasn't Spanish. Wasn't German either, which the commander figured was of some comfort. At least Nazis weren't running the show.

There was another voice, close by, giving orders. At a guess, *Generalkapitano* Araujo had come to gloat.

The door's wheel spun and it swung open. Two armed guards stepped through, holding real fancy-looking machine pistols – as artistic as the amphibious planes on the top deck – and took positions either side of the doorway. Then a third figure stepped through. A woman: tall, grey-eyed, with a mass of burnished red hair, and one hell of a smile.

There was something about her that made Munrow think of drinks on the White House lawn: a Katharine Hepburn sense of sophistication. He couldn't figure it, dressed as she was in a slightly comic opera uniform similar to Araujo's – but hers fitted a whole lot better. Looked like it cost a damned sight more too.

"Lieutenant-Commander Munrow," she said. Her voice was Hepburn, too; cut-glass, maybe even real English. "My apologies for detaining you so long in—" she cast her eyes around the too bright cabin "—such circumstances."

"I've known worse. There was this place in Boise, once—" Munrow stood up from the wall. The heavies with guns stiffened. "And you are?"

Her smile broadened. Now she reminded him of a fancy *maître d'* who was about to tell him his table wouldn't be ready for another hour. "I am *Generaladmiralo* Amaris Steele, Captain of the *La Estro*."

"You?" He didn't try to hide his surprise. "I thought that was the other guy's job."

"Araujo?" She laughed – a bright, careless sound. "No, he's what you would call my Number One. I am in overall command of our flagship. Speaking of which, what do you think of her?"

"It's a big ship," he said. "Must have cost a few bucks."

"She wasn't cheap, I'll admit."

"From the Nazis?"

"Ah – you would have seen the deputation. The *Generalkapitano* was my proxy for those gentlemen. If you know anything about *Führerprinzip* you can imagine how seriously they would treat a woman leader. We do not have such prejudices, of course." Her smile faltered for a moment. "You saw the aircraft in which they left. Quaint, out of date. You think they could have launched this?" She swept an arm in an inclusive gesture. "Or *La Barba Vulturo*?"

For a moment Munrow was baffled. "The big flying boat?"

"Exactly. Germany will be buying from *us*, commander – not the other way around."

"Even though the *Luftwaffe* guy wasn't happy about you attacking my sub."

"The *USS Oswin*? Don't look so surprised, commander. The submarine cruiser club is a very exclusive one. There is no vessel presently afloat to match your submarine's length and profile." She shook her head and sighed. "The pilot was young, eager. He wanted to show off – give those two gentlemen a real show. He was never to have flown anywhere near your submarine. Once he did, of course, he thought he should correct his mistake."

"And nearly got shot down for his trouble."

The *Generaladmiralo* stepped closer. Munrow could smell her scent. "I can assure you, *La Barba Vulturo* was in no danger from your anti-aircraft fire, commander."

"We still hurt it. Bet the Nazi brass wasn't happy about nearly ending up in the drink."

She stared around at the cabin walls. "*La Estro* is a floating city, commander, the first of many. The *Flotego de Urboj* is a new concept in world government: effectively city-states able to roam at will across most of the globe's surface. Capable of defending themselves against all aggression, whilst free to retaliate."

"Surprised the Nazis are happy with that."

"They might have the land, eventually, but we shall have the oceans. You see—" her smile returned "—they need us. They have little oil for fuel – we have more than enough."

Munrow was beginning to work it out. "You sell them oil, use the money to build a big crazy flying boat and a ship the size of an island, tell the Nazis you can do the same for them if they have the green, and relieve them of a few hundred thousand grand—"

"Millions, darling." Her smile turned predatory. "Elegant, isn't it."

"Not what I'd call it." He leaned against the bulkhead again. "So who did build this big tub, and that flying leviathan?"

"Citizens of the world, commander. A global concern. This is why we have chosen Esperanto as our *lingua franca*."

"That what all the signs are in?"

"Language is nationalist, commander. A constructed language has no borders."

"Huh. So what happens to me now? My men?"

"For now you are our guests, until we decide what to do with you. You can't return to your submarine, of course. We may already have sunk it—"

Munrow laughed. "You expect me to swallow that?"

"—and I for one would hate to see you thrown overboard."

He wondered if that's what they'd done with the flying boat's overkeen pilot. "Wouldn't be so happy myself."

"Quite." She turned about. Stepping through the door she paused and glanced back. "I'll have some refreshments sent to you and your men."

"Thank you – admiral."

"A brave new world, commander. Get used to it."

She walked away. The two armed guards backed through the doorway and secured it. Munrow was left alone again.

He smacked his first against the bulkhead. He had to get out, find his boys, and return to the *Oswin*. If she hadn't been sunk, if she was still following the big ship in the dark. He refused to accept she wasn't still afloat, still active. For his own sanity, at least.

He paced the cabin, running hands over the smooth walls. As he passed the door one hand brushed against the descending pipes. He flinched: one was hot.

He stepped closer, examining them, scraping at the paint with a thumbnail. It peeled easily, revealing the red-gold metal underneath. Copper. Copper was malleable, especially when hot. If he could find a joint...

He ran a finger down each pipe, careful not to burn himself on the hot one. He felt the joint more than saw it, about three feet above the deck. In the hot pipe. It figured.

He tugged at it. The metal was far too hot for him to hold for more than a few seconds.

Munrow slipped off his belt and ran it around the pipe twice, just below the joint. Wrapping the free ends around his wrists and hands, he pulled. Did the pipe move a fraction? He braced his left foot against the smooth bulkhead wall and hauled on the belt again. The pipe moved a little more. Munrow grasped the belt tighter, gritting his teeth, and heaved.

The pipe split. Steam hissed lazily. Munrow hauled on his belt again. This time the whole joint fractured. The pipe bent away from the wall, steam gushing from the broken end. After a moment the pressure dropped a little. The commander stepped aside, then bore down on the jutting length of pipe with one foot, putting his weight behind it. It bent a little. He heaved on it again. It bent further, almost sticking out at a right angle. Munrow stamped on it once more, hard, forcing the broken end to the floor. He peeled off his shirt, wrapping it around the hot pipe, and began to work the metal – up and down, across. With each heave the pipe moved more freely, hosing low-pressure steam into the air.

Suddenly the stressed metal tore. Munrow straightened, clutching over two feet of cooling, jagged-ended pipe. Steam boiled out of a stump just above floor level. Likely to get a bit tropical in here soon, he thought.

The locking wheel turned with a faint rattle. As the door swung open Munrow ducked behind it. A hand, supporting a small tray, appeared. Munrow seized the wrist and pulled it as hard as he had the pipe. A guard stumbled through the doorway, slamming against the opposite bulkhead. The tray hit the deck, scattering its contents. Munrow stepped around the door, coming face to face with another guard, this one armed.

Munrow swung his crude sap, catching the guard across the neck. The man staggered, dropping the machine pistol he'd been cradling. Before the guard could recover, Munrow half dragged, half threw him through the doorway into the small room, slamming the door shut and spinning the wheel. It locked with a simple twin-catch mechanism.

Pausing only to pull on his belt and crumpled shirt, Munrow discarded his length of copper pipe and picked up the fancy machine pistol. He headed off along the passageway.

At the end was an open stairwell. He heard footsteps and a voice. He flattened himself against a bulkhead, willing whoever it was to go someplace else. *Generalkapitano* Araujo came around a corner, in conversation with two armed guards. If anyone knew where Vallone and the rest were, it'd be him.

Munrow stepped into view, levelling his machine pistol. "Hold it. All of you."

Maybe one of the guards didn't understand, maybe he didn't think the bedraggled commander was much of a threat. He raised his own weapon. Munrow opened fire. His machine pistol spat a stream of bullets with a curious, high-pitched whine. The guard spun off his feet, dropping his weapon, and hit the floor. Munrow sprinted forward, grabbing Araujo by his high collar, and aimed his gun at the second guard.

"Tell your boy to play nice, or he gets the same!"

Araujo spoke. The guard nodded, his eyes promising murder the first chance he got.

"Now you're going to take me to wherever my men are locked up. Tell laughing boy to leave his gun on the deck, that he's going in front, and add I'll have no problem shooting him in the back if I have to. Got it?"

"You'll never reach the—"

Munrow twisted his grip. "You'd better pray we do, *generalkapitano*, because I can guarantee you'll die first. Tell him!"

The guard nodded again at Araujo's orders. He placed his machine pistol on the floor, watching Munrow closely. The commander crouched, pulling Araujo down with him as he slung his stolen gun across a shoulder and snatched up the two on the deck. He slung one alongside the first, keeping the third ready in his left hand. Then he indicated the guard should move toward the companionway. Arm tight around Araujo's throat, choking back any attempt to call out, Munrow followed.

The descending companionway had high rails running down bulkheads on both sides. If Araujo made any attempt to trip them up, Munrow was pretty confident he could land on the *kapitano* – breaking his fall, if nothing else.

They came out on the open upper flight deck with all the sleek amphibs. His cell must have been up at around the same height as the arched beams over the deck. Seemed like this ship went off forever. And they hadn't seen any other member of the *La Estro's* crew yet. They all in cold storage or something? And what was this ship's complement? Did it operate semi-automatically?

"Where we heading?"

"The main port bulkhead door," Araujo wheezed.

They crossed the flight deck, weaving through the stationary airplanes. Munrow's attention was split between Araujo and the guard, alert for one of them trying to make a break for it among the amphibs, while looking out for any other crew members who might suddenly materialise.

Araujo nodded his head towards a door in the side bulkhead. "Through there," he gasped past Munrow's tight hold round his neck.

"Fine." The commander waved his machine pistol at the guard. "After you." Adding to Araujo, "Tell him I'm itching for him to do something stupid."

The *generalkapitano* hissed something. The guard spat back a reply, not happy. Munrow hoped Araujo wasn't trying to be smart. He gestured with the gun again. The guard stepped through the doorway. Munrow pushed Araujo after him, not letting either out of sight.

"Here." Araujo nodded awkwardly towards a closed door. The wheel was dogged by the twin catch device.

Munrow stared at the door. "My boys are in there?"

Araujo nodded.

That made no sense. "Why keep us so far apart?"

The *generalkapitano* shrugged. "*Generaladmiralo* Steele's orders. She wanted you spread about the ship, not all in the same place. We were about to split up your crew." He smiled. "You are lucky."

"I sleep with a rabbit's foot." That admiral is one smart cookie, thought Munrow. If they'd been scattered about the carrier it would have taken much longer to find them. Too bad for her Araujo wasn't so sharp. "Tell your boy to open it."

Araujo gave a short order. The guard, after a pause during which Munrow thought he wasn't going to obey, unsecured the door and opened it.

"Inside," ordered Munrow. If there were more of Araujo's men inside, the commander would know pretty soon. If it was the chief and his boys ... well, Munrow could guess at the reception a lone, unarmed guard would get.

The guard stepped inside. A moment later there was a yell followed by a dull thud. The door swung back further, revealing Chief Vallone, Slade and Caetano. The guard was on the floor, still. Vallone's face split into a wide grin when he saw Munrow.

"Commander! Boy am I happy it's you!" He spared Araujo a glance. "What's the plan?"

"To get the hell out of here and warn the *Oswin*." He slipped the two fancy machine pistols off his shoulder, handing one each to Vallone and Caetano. Then he kicked Araujo into the makeshift brig and secured the door behind him.

"Chief, how many flying hours have you logged?"

Vallone frowned. "Just thirty-two in total, commander."

"Think you could manage one of those amphibs?"

They stepped onto the flight deck. The chief scanned the nearest sesquiplane. Munrow had seen him happier.

"I guess so, sir. A plane's a plane." He rubbed at his chin. "Getting aloft might be a problem, though."

Munrow looked back and forth. Like the deck below, this was sealed at both ends by bulkheads. Moveable ones, he figured. "Assuming all these kites are pointing forward, and that we get the doors open, with this bucket's headway and the plane opened right up we should get airborne."

"Maybe." Vallone face didn't lighten up any. "I figure this deck's higher than the *Lexington's*, and those kites don't look too heavy." He frowned. "Anything above sixty knots should get one in the air."

"Very well. Get on board the leading plane and prep for take-off. I'll see about getting the front gate open."

Vallone, Slade and Caetano hopped aboard one amphib that was forward of the rest. There was half a flight deck laid out in front, and Munrow hoped whoever had lined the airplanes up had been smart enough to give them space to take off. If they hadn't it was going to be a short flight.

He hurried forward and searched the end bulkhead for something to spring the forward doors open. He figured each deck had to have separate controls; or at least, he hoped so. After a minute or so he came across a large interlocking lever with the sign *Malfermu Ĉiuj Ferdekaj Pordoj* and a picture of what looked like a half-open gate above it. It looked promising.

"Here goes nothing."

Munrow pulled on the lever. It moved smoothly. He shoved it down as far as it would go. There was a thud and distant whine. Glancing up, Munrow saw the forward deck end was gradually lowering, forming an extension to the flight deck.

Bullets ricocheted off the bulkhead to his right. Armed guards were advancing forward along the ship's port bulkhead. All we carrying those fancy machine pistols. A couple were firing. The commander's luck had finally run out.

Munrow was pinned down, exposed. This time there were no fuel drums to dodge behind. He brought up his own gun and returned fire. One guard went down. After a moment his weapon's strange whining fire stopped. Out of ammo he guessed.

More gunfire echoed across the flight deck: the boys onboard the lead amphib. A heavy machine gun in the port side was spraying lead. Caetano was on his belly under the landing gear, firing back with his own sleek gun. Heart in his mouth, Munrow tossed his empty weapon aside and ran for it.

It was over quickly. The plane's machine gun made short work of the carrier's crewmen. Before the echoes had died its twin engines coughed, whined, then roared to life. Munrow reached the airplane. He ducked, snatching at the nearest wheel chocks, pulling them out from the machine's left wheel. Caetano did the same with the right. The commander was about to stand when he noticed a long, sleek black shape inset into the amphib's keel.

He came to his feet, reaching for the half-open cabin door. Movement above him caught his eye. A lone figure was standing in a railed gallery high on the internal port bulkhead. It was *Generaladmiralo* Steele. Amaris. She looked down and blew a kiss, then stepped out of sight.

He climbed into the plane's spacious cabin, Caetano close behind him. A keen wind cut through his damp shirt. Just visible behind the ranks of amphibs he could see the deck's aft doors were also dropping open.

Munrow dropped into the pilot seat next to Vallone. His heart was still racing, and it took him a moment before he could speak. "You ready, Chief?"

"As I'll ever be, sir."

"Don't hang around for my sake."

Vallone opened up the engines. The plane vibrated, eager to surge forward.

"What we waiting for?" asked Munrow. He checked left and right, expecting more armed men to come pouring onto the deck any moment.

"This bird has brakes, Commander." Vallone's face was creased with worry. "Damned if I can figure out the off lever!"

Caetano leaned between them. "I'm guessing that one, chief!" He stabbed a finger at a small switch.

"I hope you're right." Vallone palmed the switch, and the plane lurched forward. Engines wide open, it headed for the open door, bouncing like it was eager to get off the ground.

Munrow heard gunfire. "Shut that up, will you."

From behind came the hammer of the cabin's rear machine guns. The external gunfire fell silent.

The plane was right at the lip of the extended flight deck. It kept going. Munrow's guts leapt towards the plane's cabin roof as its nose abruptly dipped. The chief pulled back on the yoke, hissing a stream of cuss words. The nose came up. The plane levelled off. Around twenty feet above the ocean it took to the air.

Munrow started breathing again. He looked out his window, watching the huge vessel dropping away below them. It was still dark, but from above even the flight deck's dim lighting lit it up like Macey's.

He let out a shaky whistle of relief and ran his eye over the control panel.

"I have two questions. Did anyone else notice the torpedo under this bird? And would you know how to drop it?"

◌

The talker phone buzzed. Captain Bannon picked it up.

"Bridge, this is hydrophones. I'm picking up something odd-sounding, Captain. Directly ahead."

"Odd how?"

"Chattering noise. Staccato. It's faint, but distinct from the target's engine sounds."

"Gunfire?"

"Possibly, sir."

"Very well." Probably Brad and his party making themselves a nuisance, Bannon thought. "Sound general quarters."

"General quarters, aye."

Bannon hung up the phone. Ahead, the horizon was a black line against dawn's approach. That huge ship would be clearly visible pretty soon. The captain hoped Brad was in a shape to appreciate their help.

∞

The amphib made a slow, clumsy turn. Vallone was still getting a feel for the controls. So far, no other plane had come after them.

Munrow ran through the plane's offensive capabilities. "Twin nose cannon, fired by either pilot or co-pilot." There was a button on the yoke in front of him. He couldn't fly worth a damn, but he knew how to shoot. "Port and starboard heavy machine guns." Manned by Slade and Caetano in the cabin's rear. "And a torpedo slung under the keel." It was a pretty formidable set-up. "We know the guns are loaded – can we make the same assumption about the torpedo?"

Vallone glanced his way. "You'll need more than one fish to sink that baby, Commander."

Munrow grinned. "I don't intend to try, Chief. But wouldn't you say a torpedo – dropped on a flight deck – would make one hell of a mess?"

"Like a bomb, sir?" Vallone looked doubtful.

"Only one way to find out. Take us back."

"Commander?"

"That's an order, Chief."

"Aye, sir." Vallone turned the amphib and steered back towards the *La Estro*. The massive ship hadn't changed course and still had to launch more planes. Munrow wondered if they were short of pilots as well as crew. Maybe they had just enough to sail the carrier and impress the Nazis. Made him wonder just how big the admiral's organisation really was.

"Overfly by around a hundred feet, keeping our speed down low as you can. I want to drop that fish right in the middle of her top deck."

Vallone sighed. "If you say so, Commander."

The plane approached the *La Estro* from its stern. A luminescent wash boiled in its wake. Huge gun turrets in the upper superstructure were rotating in the plane's direction, triple barrels elevating. Munrow wondered if his plan was even dumber than he'd first thought.

"Commander!"

"I see it, Chief. Guns that size are for hitting battleships, not a kite like this." I hope, he added silently.

"Maybe so, sir – but they'll have AA guns among them."

Tracer began to drift up from the *La Estro's* ramparts. None of it came close to the amphib, but the chief twitched the plane nervously across the sky anyway. "Me and my big mouth," he muttered.

The plane flew over the vessel's stern, fireflies of tracer flashing against the dim sky.

"Get that torpedo ready," said Munrow.

Vallone reached below the flight controls and after a moment eased back on a lever. "If any of you are the praying kind, I'd appreciate a kind word or two."

Below, one of the huge guns fired all barrels. There was no smoke – just a howl which Munrow heard above the plane's engines. The small amphib lurched in the wake of three shells screaming invisibly past.

"What the hell are they using?" Vallone's face was slick with sweat. "Rubber bands?"

"Drop that fish," said Munrow. "And pray."

The chief sounded like he was praying himself as he tugged on another lever. The amphib bobbed as the torpedo's weight was abruptly lost. "Whaddya know, it worked!"

Vallone turned the yoke and pushed more power to the engines. The plane banked aside, accelerating even as it climbed. The steams of tracer fell behind. Two more turret guns howled, but the shells went wide.

As the plane turned, Munrow craned in his seat, watching through the cabin's port windows. Below, the La Estro shuddered as the torpedo hit the top deck, exploding on impact. The blast spread upward, taking out the overhead support beams. The bow and stern doors were still open: smoke and debris rolled from the vessel's ends.

Slade let go a cheer.

"Stow that," said Munrow. "We might have stung that monster, but it's far from hurt."

"How about a strafing run?" said Caetano. "If the chief's up to it."

Munrow glanced at Vallone's strained expression. "Well, Chief?"

Vallone's mouth twitched in a ghastly grin. "Sure – it'll be just like buzzing Wrigley Field."

Munrow laughed. "Then if you two back there are ready?"

Vallone turned the plane once more, flying parallel to the *La Estro*. He seemed to be getting a handle on the kite. The huge ship was still making headway, despite the thick black smoke rolling off the top deck. The torpedo had just scratched it.

Overtaking the ship, Vallone banked the amphib and turned it straight towards the gaping bow doors. Munrow wondered how long before they'd be shut again. Maybe the fire would keep the crew distracted.

The smoking flight deck neared at unnerving speed. It was littered by the wreckage of shattered or partly destroyed airplanes. Crewman ran chaotically. Munrow wondered where Amaris Steele was.

"Give 'em hell, boys," Munrow said as the amphib swooped towards the deck opening. He began firing the forward cannons. From behind he heard the heavy rattle of machine guns. There was no time to see what effect their crazy flight was having: the amphib soared over the shattered deck, firing lead indiscriminately, and shot out of the stern in what felt like a moment.

As Vallone pulled the amphib into a climb, Slade and Caetano gave the *La Estro* a parting spray of shells. Munrow looked back. The top deck was a mess: damaged planes even more shot up, bodies strewn about. Everything half-shrouded by black smoke.

Vallone gave a quiet whoop. "It's the *Oswin!*"

Munrow looked ahead. There was the sub, her hull and superstructure glowing orange in the rays of a sun hauling itself over the horizon. The commander began to smile in relief. The smile froze when he saw the v-winged shape looming in the sky, just to the *Oswin's* stern. The massive flying boat. Coming straight at them both.

CঞৎৎO

The sun seemed to lurch up abruptly, casting reddish light across the still black sea. Ahead of the *Oswin*, the huge carrier glowed orange in the sunrise. The ship was still underway, but there was obviously something wrong. Captain Bannon couldn't make out any flames, but thick smoke curled around the massive superstructure, black against the purple sky.

A small plane skimmed the waves, coming straight for the *Oswin*, sunlit as garishly as the huge vessel. It sped past the sub at almost zero feet, waggling its wings, grazing the waves with a wingtip. Bannon had no time to see who was flying the machine, but his gut told him it had to be one of Brad's boys. On impulse he waved, turning to watch the plane climb back into the dawn sky.

Which was when he saw the other airplane, high up, still distant, its sheer size making it stand out. That damned flying ocean liner!

And Brad was obviously intent on taking the thing on.

CঞৎৎO

Munrow watched the flying boat filling the cabin's windshield. They were a dogfish taking on a killer whale.

Chief Vallone whistled. "That's one big son of a bitch!"

Munrow had forgotten the chief hadn't seen the *La Barba Vulturo* the first time around. "The bigger they come," he said.

"I guess." Vallone took them closer. Tracer began flashing from the flying boat's twin hulls. Both Munrow and the chief pressed the buttons on their flying yokes, returning fire. It was hard to tell if any of the shells hit.

"Go for the engines," said Munrow. "The *Oswin's* AA fire managed to hit a couple last time. If we can take out enough that flying whale should lose its wings."

"Right with you, Commander." Vallone steered the amphib up and over the huge plane, out of reach of its forward guns. Two more opened up from the V-wing's trailing edge. The chief jinked their plane left and right, trying to avoid the streams of tracer.

Munrow kept his eye on the gunsight in the window before him, firing short bursts every time any part of the flying boat flicked across it. Vallone was flying their ship like he'd done nothing else since the day he was born. The commander would definitely be recommending the guy for his wings once they were out of this jam.

An engine came into range. Munrow fired. Chunks of a rear prop flew past the amphib. From the rear of the cabin came the sound of a machine gun. Somebody let out a breathless whoop.

As Vallone brought the amphib round, swooping back along the flying boat's wing, Munrow saw oily streamers from two of the engines. "Just another twenty or so to go," he muttered.

There was more gunfire from the cabin gunners. For a moment, the amphib was enveloped in black cloud.

"Two more, Commander!" Slade called, all excited.

Vallone settled the amphib onto the flying boat's tail. All of the engines were now in range – but so were they. Guns on the main wing's trailing edge had a clear shot. The chief side-slipped out of the way.

"It's well-defended, Commander. The engines are the weak point, but any approach, aside from flying back and forth parallel to the wing, exposes us to fire. And even then I figure somebody might get a bead."

Munrow stared at the flying hulk, seeming to flit past his vision as the chief flew the amphib around it, dodging shells. "What about the cockpit?"

Vallone frowned at him. "A front-on approach will put us right in line with the forward gunners."

"Who said anything about front-on?"

CR&D

A geyser erupted in the ocean, ten yards off the *Oswin's* starboard bow, sparkling yellow in the sun's horizontal rays.

Bannon ducked instinctively as fine spray flew across the forward deck. He looked up at the huge vessel before them, checking for gun smoke. He saw nothing.

Another fountain erupted to port – less than ten yards off.

He grabbed the talker. "Manoeuvring, full reverse. Battle stations. Gun and torpedo action."

As the stations acknowledged the order, Bannon grabbed his binoculars. The rising sun highlighted the huge vessel's cityscape superstructure in stark light and shadow. The smoke seemed to be thinning. It took the captain several seconds to take in the sheer size of the gun turrets. Carefully nestled among the tower blocks they looked even bigger than those on the old Great War dreadnoughts he remembered. As he watched one of the turrets seemed to twitch. A fine mist curled up from it. Three seconds later a shell ploughed into the sea, no more than ten yards directly in front of the sub's prow. They were getting the range – and the *Oswin* still couldn't dive.

"Gunnery officer. Target that ship. Return fire."

"*Gunnery officer, aye.*"

The sub's turret rotated slowly, twin barrels raising. A moment later it fired. Two eight-inch shells arced towards the target. They slammed in broadside, to little effect.

"Cease fire," ordered Bannon. "Manoeuvring, keep us off their port beam, bow forward. Give them as narrow a target as possible." While we give them all we got, he added.

"*Manoeuvring, aye.*"

"Forward room, order of tubes is one, three."

"*One, three, aye.*"

The sea geysered up on either side of the sub's hull, both impacts wide by over ten yards. Bannon glanced up to the skies. He couldn't see the small seaplane; had it been hit, he wondered. The flying boat looked to be in trouble, or maybe that was wishful thinking. Either way, he could see sunlight-tinted streams of smoke trailing from the massive airplane.

Another shell ploughed into the ocean, too close. Seawater drenched him.

"Forward room. Set depth zero eight feet. Fire one and three."

೧೮೮ಲ

The amphib climbed rapidly. Up and forward of the flying boat. Munrow couldn't see the other plane from his seat any longer, and he sure hoped Vallone knew what he was doing.

The amphib levelled off. Dipping a wing slightly, the chief glanced down. "Well, Commander. Here goes nothing." He managed a weak smile.

"All for one, Chief."

Vallone turned the dip into a turn, dropping the nose. The turn became a dive. Munrow could see the flying boat now, steady even though several engines were leaking smoke. As far as the commander could tell, Chief Vallone had them on a perfect intercept course.

The glasshouse cockpit grew larger. The amphib was aimed straight for it. Tracer rose up from the flying boat's guns, but the small plane was moving too fast, presenting too small a target. All of the gunfire went wide.

Munrow concentrated on his target. Beside him, the chief seemed just as intent. The cockpit grew from a network of glass panels to distinct panes. Munrow could almost count the number of frames holding it together.

"Now, chief!"

They both hit their firing buttons. The forward cannons hammered. The flying boat's cockpit windows shattered. Chunks of framework flew apart.

Then the amphib was below the V wing, turning.

The cabin shuddered. Glass splintered. The sound of the amphib's twin engines grew louder, harsher. The plane flipped. Vallone hauled on his yoke, swearing under his breath. After more seconds than Munrow wanted to count, the amphib straightened up.

Munrow relaxed in his seat. "Everybody okay?"

The chief nodded. Slade called out, "Caetano caught a chunk of glass in his arm."

"I'm fine," said Caetano. "You oughta see the other guy."

Munrow glanced out a window. He could see the flying boat, no longer steady, drifting into a shallow dive. One that grew steeper by degrees.

"Gentlemen, I think we did it."

Above him the amphib's engines gave a final, anguished cough, and fell silent.

୧୬

A fourth torpedo detonated against the huge ship's shadowed hull. Checking through his glasses, Bannon couldn't see if the vessel was so much as scratched.

"Forward room, reload tubes one, two, three."

"Forward room, aye."

Shells impacted the ocean to either side of the *Oswin's* hull. Spray washed over the decks. The sub's narrow, end on profile might be harder to target, but the high turrets were gradually getting closer.

A crazy idea struck Bannon. "Manoeuvring, take us in closer."

"Captain?"

"Get under their guns. They can only lower those barrels so far."

"Getting closer, aye."

"Forward room ready,"

"Fire one and three."

The fish sped across the ocean, leaving a pale, phosphorescent wake. They impacted the ship's hull, throwing tons of water into the air. Far as Bannon could tell, the massive hulk barely twitched.

"Fire two."

The huge ship was filling more of the captain's vision as the *Oswin* crept closer. He never heard a shot, but the shriek of rounds passing close by was unnerving. The sub was closing faster than the ship could lower its guns, but each volley fell worryingly close to stern.

The third torpedo struck. The ocean erupted.

"Forward room, reload..."

Another volley screamed overhead. Bannon had to fight the urge to duck. The rounds hit the water, some twenty yards astern of the sub.

All Bannon could see now was the towering ship. it dominated his senses. He never imagined vessels reaching such a size.

"Forward room, fire when ready."

"Captain!" It was the rear lookout, just behind Bannon on the bridge. "Plane, sir. Coming in."

Bannon turned. Up in the paling sky was a lumbering shape, dropping rapidly, black trails of smoke billowing from its engines, tracing an arc as its dive gradually steepened. The flying boat. Brad and his boys must have brought it down.

But it was going to hit uncomfortably close. And that flying boat would plough an awful big hole in the ocean.

"Forward room, belay that order. Manoeuvring, all back full."

The *Oswin* slowed, stopped, and began to reverse. Away from the huge ship, but back in range of its guns.

"Gunnery officer, recommence firing. Target is those turrets." Might as well go out fighting.

The lookout pointed again. "Another plane, sir. Smaller."

The captain saw it. Moving too fast to get a fix with his glasses, but he knew it was the small amphib he'd seen earlier. Also coming in straight for the water.

"Keep an eye on it, mister. We'll need to pick up survivors." If we survive ourselves, he didn't add.

Plumes of water began to fountain around the sub as it backed into the gun's sights. The *Oswin's* own deck gun returned fire. Bannon kept his eye on the flying boat, trying to figure just how close they'd be when it hit.

The plane was close enough for him to hear the whine of its engines. More smoke streamed back from its angled wing. One of the engines broke free and spun towards the water. The flying boat yawed to the right and rolled, starboard wingtip dipping. With a final drunken spin it ploughed into the huge ship's stern. It exploded, hurling deadly chunks of metal skywards. Fuel ignited into a colossal fireball, spraying liquid flame fore and aft. Some arced in the direction of the retreating *Oswin*, leaving burning patches on the waves.

"Manoeuvring, slow to one third."

There was another explosion aboard the ship. This time Bannon was pretty sure it shuddered. Flames billowed out of the stern. More debris followed.

"Launch the second motorboat," Bannon ordered the lookout, watching as an inferno slowly engulfed the huge vessel. Lord knew what the ship had on board to create such a firestorm, so quickly. "Direct it to wherever that second plane came down." And pray they made it.

"Aye, sir. And the ... ship we engaged?"

Bannon stared at it. Thick oily smoke poured in a choking cloud from inside. Deep within the hull came a succession of explosions, each one shaking the vessel to the waterline. It had started to list. Either the flying boat's impact had caused fatal damage, or finished off whatever the *Oswin's* torpedoes had started.

"We'll pick up survivors."

ಃ௠

The Oswin hung around searching for as long as they dared, but the lookouts spotted nothing in the water from either the carrier or the flying boat. No bodies, no survivors. Not so much as a damaged life raft to hint that anyone had escaped. When the burning ship finally sank, creating a swell that made the sub's four-hundred-foot-long hull bob like a cork, it was assumed everyone had gone down with it.

Bannon visited Munrow in his cabin. The commander had changed out of his wet clothes and was half-lying on his bunk, smoking and drinking coffee, a sleek, odd-looking gun in his lap.

"A souvenir?" asked Bannon.

Munrow handed it over. "Some kind of machine pistol, or submachine gun. Like a Thompson designed by Emperor Ming."

The captain hefted the sleek black weapon. "Standard equipment on board that big tug?"

Munrow nodded. "Powered by electricity, or magnetism, or something just as crazy. We'll never know for sure – seawater jazzed it for good."

"Well, maybe the boys back home can figure it out." He tossed it back onto the bunk.

"How's Caetano?" asked Munrow, stubbing out his cigarette.

"Complaining endlessly, so I guess he's fine. Slade and the chief just swallowed a bit of seawater."

"That's something."

"I understand the antenna's finally been fixed, so we can tell the folks back home all about the holes that need patching. I'm also looking forward to your report."

"You'll never believe it."

"We just sunk a ship the size of Central Park, Brad. I'm almost prepared to believe anything."

Munrow picked up the strange machine pistol and turned it over. His eyes had a faraway look. "Keep that in mind when you read it, huh?"